I0679146

This work is fiction. All characters and incidents are the product of the author's imagination or are used in a fictitious manner. Any resemblance to persons living or dead or to any actual incident or event is purely coincidental.

Published in the USA.

1

Acknowledgments

I would like to thank all of our friends who have been instrumental in developing this book. They have been inspirational and supportive. I would like to thank a few people who were key in reviewing *Our Secret Life: Awakening* and providing constructive feedback in its development.

Thank you:

KA

BG

KG

JC

VO

Chapter 1: The Beginning

Ginger

I savored the rare moment of solitude as I strolled through the mall. My footsteps echoed off the polished floors and glass storefronts, the soft glow of sunlight filtering through the skylights. The displays gleamed invitingly, each one a siren call of fashion and elegance.

Gazing longingly at the beautiful clothes and accessories behind the windows, I felt an insistent pull. Something tugged at my senses, urging me to explore further. The rich, tantalizing aroma of freshly brewed coffee drew me into a crowded café. I ordered my favorite caramel macchiato latte and continued through the bustling mall.

A few steps later, an artist captured my attention in the walkway. He was creating a stunning portrait. Mesmerized, I settled onto a nearby bench, sipped my latte and watched him work. Soon something else caught my eye: a pamphlet lying innocuously on the bench beside me, featuring a couple embracing on its cover. My curiosity piqued, I picked it up and examined it more closely.

To my surprise—and mild embarrassment—it turned out to be an advertisement for an adult novelty store. My cheeks flushed with warmth as I quickly set it back down and nervously glanced around. No one seemed to notice. Tentatively, I opened the pamphlet again, flipping through the glossy pages filled with vibrators, handcuffs, and other risqué items. Intrigue mingled with unease as my heart fluttered in anticipation.

My fingers paused on a familiar shape—Ryan's manhood replicated in a lifelike vibrator. Heat flooded my body at the thought of using such a toy in place of Ryan, but anxiety quickly followed. What if he came home unexpectedly and found it? How would I explain it to him? What if my kids found it?

Two elderly women interrupted my thoughts as they walked by and greeted me. Feeling like a teenager caught with a naughty magazine, I quickly closed the pamphlet and hid it in my lap. Cheeks burning with embarrassment, I cheerily replied to their greeting and discreetly scanned the area for onlookers. With a deep breath, I opened the pamphlet again, only to close it just as quickly. The anticipation was too much to bear, and I couldn't wait until Ryan returned home from his military deployment to satisfy our desires without the need for any toys or novelties.

As the week drew to a close, and my children were off to school, I set about my usual routine of cleaning the house. Today, though, I had the sudden urge to switch out the contents of my purse. It was time to retire my old one and embrace the new purchase from my mall trip—a sleek black leather handbag that exuded sophistication.

I unzipped the pockets of my trusty old purse and dumped its contents onto my neatly made bed. Sorting through the items, I noticed something stuck at the bottom. With a smile, I reached in and retrieved it. To my surprise, it was the pamphlet from the mall. Heat rose to my cheeks again as an unexpected giddiness bubbled up inside me. How silly it seemed to hide this small thing—yet, there was a thrill in keeping it a secret.

4

With a mischievous grin, I glanced around the room before unfolding the pamphlet. My gaze devoured each page until I came face-to-face with that unmistakable vibrator. The memory of Ryan's touch surged again, igniting a deep ache within me. The lifelike details—every vein and subtle curve—stirred my core with an undeniable hunger. There was no doubt about it: I needed it.

Embarrassment threatened to hold me back, but I gave in to my desires. After all, who would know except for me? With determination, I tore out the mail-order form on the back page and carefully selected the item I wanted. As I sealed the envelope and placed it with payment inside the mailbox, a blush tinged my cheeks at the thought of what awaited me.

After what felt like an eternity, the long-awaited package finally arrived in the mail. My heart raced with excitement as I hastily made my way upstairs, eager to open my new present. I couldn't help but feel a tinge of teenaged rebellion as I carefully peeled back the packaging, trying not to make too much noise and risk getting caught.

And there it was, my new pleasure device. With a shaky hand, I traced my fingers over its length, marveling at the intricate veins and curves that seemed almost lifelike. It was like exploring a new lover for the first time. The thought of how it would feel inside me sent shivers down my spine.

As I held it in my hands and felt its weight, it became all too real. After inserting the batteries and turning it on, I was taken aback by the intense vibrations that radiated through my body. Placing the vibrating toy against my leg caused a rush of desire to spread throughout me, leaving me flushed and trembling with need.

After quickly returning it to its box and hiding it away in my dresser drawer, I couldn't shake off the overwhelming urge to try it out again.

#

A few days later, while putting away laundry, I couldn't resist opening the drawer and gazing upon the tantalizing box once more. Despite being alone in the house, nerves washed over me as I gently opened the lid. Reminding myself that it was just a simple toy, I took a deep breath and gripped it firmly in my hand before making my way to bed.

Sitting on the edge of the mattress, I bit my lip nervously as I stared at the device in my hand. Why was I so anxious? It was just a toy meant for pleasure. But despite my rational thoughts, shame lingered in the back of my mind. Ignoring the nagging feeling, I reminded myself that it was okay to indulge in some alone time.

I slowly explored the sensations that the toy elicited. As the pleasure built within me, all thoughts of shame vanished and were replaced with pure bliss. Perhaps this little toy wasn't just a simple object after all, but a gateway to my own pleasure and self-discovery.

As I lay on the bed, my panties inched off my hips as if they had a mind of their own. My legs parted, and I reached for the toy beside me. A simple flick of a switch, and it came to life in my hand. I felt an immediate ache deep within me. I lowered the toy and touched my sensitive flesh just below my mound, a hairline of light separating it from my clit.

A surge of electricity shot through me as the vibrating head touched my sensitive spot. My body spasmed with pleasure, quickly building toward an intense orgasm. I pressed harder. Before I could even process what was happening, my body tightened and released in waves of ecstasy. Was it the vibration? The absence of Ryan and his touch? Or perhaps the excitement and naughtiness of using this forbidden toy?

My hand instinctively reached for the bottle of lubricant in the nightstand drawer, coating my fingers before working it into my already-aching folds. Switching on the toy again, I teased myself by sliding it through my sex, spellbound by the sight and sensation. With each thrust, my neck strained to keep watching as it penetrated me, filling me just like Ryan would. I searched for that perfect spot within me as the pressure built until it hit with intensity. It was like a miracle drug, different from Ryan but satisfying in its own way.

After indulging in multiple orgasms, I cleaned myself off in the bathroom, a sudden fear and anxiety washing over me. What had just happened? Was it cheating to use a toy? Trying to push away these irrational thoughts, I hid the toy deep in my nightstand drawer, fearing the consequences if Ryan ever found out.

But as much as I tried to convince myself that it was harmless fun, an underlying fear remained. What if I became addicted to this battery-operated boyfriend? Would Ryan no longer satisfy me? Would he think I was depraved and insatiable? These thoughts consumed me, but in order to quiet them, I made a promise to only use the toy when Ryan was gone. It would be my secret, my guilty pleasure . . . my BOB.

The days were a blur of activities, filling my time and keeping me occupied. Before I knew it, a month had passed since Ryan had left for his deployment. When he called with the disappointing news that it was extended for another month, I experienced a mix of emotions. Hearing his voice sparked a craving for him, but my irritation at the extension dampened my desire. Being a single parent to three children was already difficult enough, but a husband who was randomly deployed without a return date was a constant source of frustration.

The more I thought about it, the more my irritation grew, even as the sound of Ryan's voice made me ache with longing. Stuck in this state of arousal and irritation with no outlet left me uncomfortable.

That's when I remembered . . . Bob. With the kids at school, I finally had some time to myself. And I desperately needed to relieve the tension that Ryan's call had left me with.

I went to my nightstand, and there he was: Bob, my trusty vibrator. The moment I picked him up, a smile crept onto my face. I craved it like a drug. Maybe it was even a deep-rooted need. Stripping down to nothing, I lay on the bed and turned on the vibrator. The low hum accompanied the tingling vibration in my hand as it came to life.

Although it wasn't Ryan's touch, or even an actual penis, it still had the power to make me come—and that's exactly what I needed. I moved it leisurely over my body, starting at my forearm and gliding up my shoulder, across my collarbone, and down to my breast, where I stopped on my nipple. The sensation was electric, and my body heated up with desire. Switching to the other nipple, I added to the pleasurable sensation by imagining the thrill of a man slowly moving his cock over my body. As Bob slid over my lips, I switched it off and guided him to where I wanted him. My mystery man entered my mouth now, sliding gradually to the back of my throat as I wrapped my lips tightly around him. My tongue swirled around his head and followed along his veins, mimicking the movements of a real man. Every inch of my body was aching with need. Urgently, I reached for some lubricant and applied it to my pussy before turning on Bob again. The sensation that shot through me was intense—in that moment, I truly felt like this mystery man was about to fuck me.

The head of his cock pushed past my entrance, sliding into me with a deep, pulsating vibration that sent shivers through my body. My hips eagerly thrusted to meet each one of his movements, feeling him fill me over and over again. His cock touched and teased my G-spot with every stroke, building an intense ache between my legs until it exploded into a shuddering orgasm. With each thrust, I my inner walls clenched around Bob as waves of pleasure rolled over me.

Taking a moment to catch my breath, I pulled Bob out of me with a satisfied smile, relishing in the small quakes still coursing through my body. But as I basked in the afterglow, unexpected tears welled up in my eyes. What was I doing? The intense pleasure of imagining Bob as another man made me realize how much I missed and craved Ryan. A sense of guilt washed over me as I tossed Bob to the floor and shook off the conflicting emotions that crawled under my skin.

But even as he rolled beneath the bed, I couldn't shake the thought: Would Ryan be able to make me come like that? The question lingered in my mind, casting a shadow over the blissful moments I'd just experienced. As wonderful as Bob was, he could never replace Ryan . . . right?

#

One month later, after what seemed like an eternity, Ryan finally returned home. As soon as he walked through the door, it was like my world was made whole again.

As we spent the evening with the kids, Ryan kept throwing hungry, longing glances my way. Our time apart had only intensified our desire for each other. Once the kids were tucked away in bed, we finally had time alone to reconnect and reignite the passion between us.

While Ryan took a shower, I busied myself with setting the mood. I lit romantic candles and turned on soft, sensual music to create an atmosphere oozing with seduction. With the bedroom door locked to deter any interruptions, I stripped down to nothing and eagerly anticipated Ryan's return.

Despite my excitement, a small sliver of worry lingered in the back of my mind. Would this reunion be as amazing as my last encounter with Bob? But I pushed those thoughts aside as Ryan stepped into the room, completely nude, and radiating desire with a devilish grin on his face.

With purposeful steps, he made his way toward me, and every nerve in my body came alive in anticipation. Kneeling beside me on the bed, Ryan kissed his way up my leg, lingered at my thighs, and then trailed kisses along my stomach and teasingly brushed against the edge of my breast. Finally, his lips found their way to my neck, and my hunger grew with every caress from him.

A surge of electricity jolted through my body as his teeth grazed my neck and shoulders. Every touch sent shockwaves through me and intensified the already-overwhelming pool of wetness between my thighs. His lips made their way down to my pussy, igniting a desire within me that I'd never experienced before.

His skilled tongue explored every inch of my dripping slit. My hips arched and lifted into the air in pleasure. Not even Bob, with all his experience, could make me feel like this. The thought was unexpected, but it couldn't stop the moan that escaped my throat. Why was I thinking about Bob when Ryan was here, bringing me to new heights of ecstasy? Then I remembered: Bob was still under the bed. What if Ryan found him? But why did I refer to Bob as "him"? He was just a toy.

Focus, focus.

I tried to push the thoughts out of my mind and concentrate on Ryan's expert tongue and the intense sensations he created.

"Is everything okay?" Ryan's voice pulled me back to the present as he lightly kissed my thigh.

My lying skills were average at best, but I had to try. "Yes, baby," I panted. "Just keep doing what you're doing." My fingers tangled in his hair and urged him back between my legs.

His tongue eagerly resumed its teasing and tantalizing movements around my clit, driving my hips into a frenzy. He knew exactly how to tease and please me with each flick and swirl of his tongue. But then he added two fingers inside me, skillfully hitting all the right spots and sending me closer and closer to the edge.

Ryan slowly made his way up to kiss me deeply, fully pressing his body against mine. As if sensing my desperation, he trailed the head of his rock-hard member over my slick folds and teased at my entrance before finally sliding inside. My whole body shuddered, and my eyes fluttered closed as I surrendered to the deep pleasure coursing through me.

His voice was low and commanding. "Look into my eyes."

I obeyed and met his gaze, seeing my own desire mirrored back at me. My mouth fell open and my heart raced as his length slid inside of me, inch by inch. It had been so long since I'd felt him like this, and every part of me throbbed with pleasure.

Thoughts of Bob crept into my mind. Ryan wasn't as hard as my battery-operated boyfriend. But then Ryan's touch would bring me back to the present moment, sending shivers of ecstasy through my body with each deliberate thrust. His absence had only fueled the intensity of our reunion.

Despite Bob being a decent substitute during our time apart, Ryan was still Ryan. And now I couldn't understand why I'd ever doubted wanting him. But then a thought crossed my mind: What would it feel like to have both Bob and Ryan inside of me at the same time? I pushed the thought away, overwhelmed by the pleasure coursing through me.

"Fuck me harder," I cried out, wrapping my legs around his waist and gripping his shoulders. The sound of our bodies colliding and our heavy breathing filled the air. Each powerful thrust brought me closer to the edge, until finally, Ryan announced that he was about to come.

"Don't stop," I begged, feeling him pulsate inside of me as he released himself. The sensation sent me over the edge as well, tumbling into a state of blissful abandon. All my muscles contracted at once in unbearable pleasure.

Even after we were both spent and panting for breath, I couldn't get enough of him. "Stay inside of me," I pleaded, craving more.

As our aftershocks subsided, Ryan asked with concern in his voice, "Is everything all right?"

I could only whimper in response, stunned by the intensity of our lovemaking. "Y-yes . . . Just give me a minute."

I curled up into a fetal position, still feeling the echoes of pleasure pulsing through my body. Ryan waited patiently for me to come back to reality, his gaze filled with love and concern. I couldn't remember ever being so consumed by desire for him.

When I finally rolled over and reached out to touch his skin, I knew this reunion was everything I'd been craving and more.

A wide, genuine smile lit up his face. "What happened to you? Do I need to spend more time away from home?"

My heart fluttered at the sound of his voice, and I snuggled into his warm embrace as he lay on his back, arms wrapped tightly around me. We talked for what seemed like hours, our hands exploring each other's bodies, until we finally drifted off to sleep.

#

The next morning, I woke up with a deep sense of joy and contentment. It only amplified when I saw Ryan sleeping peacefully next to me. Feeling incredibly grateful, I decided to surprise him with breakfast before he left for work. After all, he had rocked my world last night, and the least I could do was make him some eggs and bacon.

"Someone is in a happy mood this morning," he said as he walked into the kitchen, noticing my glowing expression.

I couldn't help but flash a bright smile and a playful wink at him as I set his plate on the table. He beamed proudly at me in return. Sure, we may have had mind-blowing sex just hours ago, but now we were back into our usual routine as he finished breakfast and kissed me

14

goodbye before heading to work. It was a longer kiss than usual, and he even gave my behind a playful squeeze on his way out, making me giggle.

A couple of hours later, with the kids off to school, I resumed my daily routine: dishes, laundry, and making the bed.

As I fluffed the pillows on our neatly made bed, something suddenly dawned on me: Bob was still hiding under there. Quickly grabbing him from his hiding spot, I headed to the bathroom to clean him off. A rush of excitement filled me as I lathered soap over his smooth surface, rinsed, and dried him off. Then I took him back to my nightstand, where he rested above the open drawer in my hand. It had been a month since I'd last seen him, but yet, Bob still had a purpose.

I dropped my bathrobe to the floor and lay down on the bed. The sound of Bob coming to life in my hand sent shivers through my body. With Bob vibrating in my hand, I gently touched my thigh, closed my eyes, and let the excitement grow.

Ryan can't vibrate like this. I love Ryan, and he's real, but I enjoy both so much. Images of last night with Ryan flashed through my mind, and I slid Bob into me, finding my sweet spot the way Ryan had. My hunger for my husband grew as Bob vibrated inside of me and I slowly fucked myself.

What if Ryan and Bob were fucking me together? I closed my eyes and could almost see my orgasm looming over me.

15

"What are you doing?" Ryan's deep voice startled me, and I threw Bob aside in a panic. My heart pounded in my chest as I realized my worst nightmare had come to life—Ryan was home, and he had caught me with Bob.

"I—I'm not doing anything," I stuttered, hoping my face didn't betray the heat rising in my cheeks.

Ryan walked toward my side of the bed, his muscles rippling under his shirt. My eyes couldn't help but wander over him, even in this moment of fear and embarrassment. "What's that?" he asked, his gaze focused on Bob lying on top of the comforter next to me.

My mind raced, trying to come up with a plausible explanation for the vibrator in front of us. But words failed me as I awaited his anger.

He picked up Bob and grinned, his blue eyes sparkling with curiosity. "When did you get this?"

I stared at him, still speechless. The irrational thought of Ryan leaving me popped into my head, and I was suddenly overcome with a rush of tears. Turning my face into the pillow, I let out a small sob.

Ryan sat down beside me on the edge of the bed, concern etched on his handsome face. "Sweetie, what's the matter?"

But I couldn't stop crying, certain that his anger would show up any moment.

Buzzzzz. I heard the vibration as Ryan turned Bob on. "Damn, this thing could knock out a tooth!"

16

His comment surprised me, and I couldn't help but laugh between sobs. He put his rough hand on my arm and rolled me over closer to him. He held Bob in front of me and tilted his head with a raised eyebrow. He deserved an answer.

"I'm embarrassed you saw that," I choked out between sobs.

"Why would you be embarrassed? It could be fun."

"For you or for me?"

"For me." His words caught me off guard, and the buzzing sound stopped. Wiping tears from my eyes, I tried to focus on him, puzzled. Did he say it could be fun? Did he mean fun for me, or fun for him? He'd never asked me to do anything with his ass before. Then again, I'd never mentioned anything to him about toys, either, yet here we were. As I considered the possibilities, a surge of arousal coursed through me.

"What do you have in mind?" I asked hesitantly.

I held my breath, unsure of what to say, or expect, next.

"Not how you're probably thinking, though," he said, his voice low and seductive. Gradually, his rough hand glided along my thigh, gently pushing my legs apart. I released my breath and bit my lower lip in anticipation as he exposed my wet entrance.

Bob's buzzing started again, and Ryan caressed the tip of the vibrator against my nipple, sending shivers down my spine. He circled around each nipple before slowly trailing down my stomach. My breath hitched as he directed

17

me to open myself with my fingers—this was something new. With shaking hands, I spread myself open for him, watching his every move with a mix of curiosity and desire.

Ryan seemed both intrigued and determined as he slid Bob into me. The last of my fear melted away as pleasure took over, the toy filling me and sliding its strong vibrations over my inner hot spot. His gaze alternated between locking in mine and watching my sex. The mischievous glint in his eye, and that smirk tugging at his lips, only added to the strong sensations coursing through me.

This is crazy, I thought incredulously. *It's almost like he's watching another guy fuck me.*

But in that moment, with Ryan's skilled hands, and Bob fulfilling my every desire, I couldn't bring myself to care about anything else.

Ryan's hand moved in a steady rhythm, thrusting Bob in and out of me with increasing intensity. The sensation of my husband fucking me with another cock ignited a fire within my body. My skin was flushed and my heart raced as I surrendered to the pleasure coursing through me.

"Hold it there," Ryan commanded before hopping off the bed. With Bob still inside me, I watched as he quickly stripped off his clothes. It had only been twenty-four hours since we were last together, yet just the sight of him spiked my desire. He motioned for me to slide down toward the middle of the bed before he climbed up on top of me, straddling my face with his legs as he reached down between my thighs.

18

"Suck my cock while I keep fucking you," he instructed, his voice dripping with lust.

My mouth eagerly opened to receive his cock, and I sucked with fervor. Moans escaped my lips as Ryan took control of Bob, thrusting with more force than before. The vibrating toy was now pounding into me almost as hard as Ryan himself would. I relished the feeling of having a cock in both my mouth and pussy at the same time, my body alive with excitement. My tongue swirled around Ryan's cock, adding to the intensity of sensations. It was almost too much to handle all at once.

But then that familiar tingle built between my legs, and I couldn't hold back any longer. "I'm coming!" I exclaimed as my inner walls spasmed around Bob.

Ryan thrusted relentlessly as the orgasm washed over me. Finally, I pulled my mouth off his cock, panting heavily. "Let me catch my breath."

With a satisfied smirk, Ryan switched off Bob's vibrations and rolled onto his side next to me. But his hands didn't leave my body. Instead, he continued to fondle and tease my sensitive areas. I relaxed and caught my breath under his touch.

Then Ryan brought Bob up to my mouth and told me to open up. Part of me hesitated, unsure of what was about to happen. But the intense arousal that still pulsed through my body was enough to override any doubts. So I obliged him, parting my lips as he pushed Bob inside. Surprisingly, the taste of my own nectar was sweet and enticing. In the past, I'd never been one to perform oral sex on Ryan after intimacy. But at that moment, I was so turned on that I would have done almost anything he asked.

As Ryan slid Bob in and out of my mouth, I closed my eyes and focused on the pleasure of the moment. It felt odd to be sucking on a toy, but imagining that it was a real man only added to the thrill. When I finally opened my eyes and looked at Ryan, his expression of awe and desire made me feel powerful. My actions had put that look on his face, and it filled me with pride and satisfaction.

"Get on your hands and knees," Ryan ordered, his voice low and commanding.

I obeyed, sinking down onto the soft bed and resting my face on a plush pillow. As I spread my knees apart, I could feel his eyes burning into me, taking in every inch of my exposed body.

"Wider," he demanded, his tone firm yet enticing.

I obliged, excitement and nervousness coursing through me. His dominant presence was intoxicating.

Then, without warning, his cock slammed into my already-sensitive pussy, and I cried out in pleasure. He wasted no time in setting a punishing pace, thrusting into me with an intensity that made me grip the pillow. With each thrust, I teetered on the edge of another earthquake. Besides yesterday, it had been far too long since we'd last had sex, and it quickly reminded me how much I craved him.

But then a buzzing sensation caressed my entrance, and I looked back to see Ryan holding the vibrator against me.

20

"What are you doing?" I asked breathlessly.

"Just relax and go with it," he replied with a coy smile.

I couldn't help but let out a gasp as he inserted both his cock and the vibrator inside of me. At first it was uncomfortable—even painful—but as he began to move within me, the sensations overwhelmed me in the best way possible. My entire body trembled as he filled and stretched me with each deep thrust.

Eventually, he pulled out both himself and the vibrator, causing me to sigh with relief. But then he reached for a bottle of lube on the nightstand and applied it to both the vibrator and my backside.

Oh God, this is new territory, I thought nervously as Ryan slid his finger into my ass. It wasn't something we'd done often before, but the thought of him exploring another part of me was exhilarating.

"I—I don't think I can," I pleaded, gripping the edges of the pillow. But deep down, I was desperate for him to continue.

"You said my cock is too big, but this vibrator is smaller. Trust me," he whispered seductively.

Unable to resist his persuasion, and eager for another mind-blowing orgasm, I gave in and let him continue. In that moment, all that mattered was my infatuation with him and the pleasure he gave me. Nothing else could compare to this deep euphoria sweeping through my body.

He pushed the vibrating toy into my tight entrance, and I couldn't help but gasp as it filled me. Ryan was gentle, waiting for me to relax before easing in the rest of it. It was a different kind of fullness from traditional intercourse, but still a mix of discomfort and electrifying pleasure.

As Ryan turned on the vibrator, a jolt of intense sensation shot through my body, and I instinctively tried to move away from it. But he gripped my hips to hold me firmly in place, then thrusted himself into my drenched sex. The combination of his deep thrusts, and the pulsating vibrations of Bob inside my ass, sent me over the edge. My body shook uncontrollably as ecstasy crashed over me, and I white-knuckled the sheets as I screamed out in pure pleasure.

Even after the deep orgasm, Ryan's strong fingers continued to dig in my skin, and he continued to pound into me. Every nerve ending was alive and tingling with desire as he brought me to climax again and again.

When it was all over, we collapsed onto the bed together. Ryan chuckled and said, "That was like having two men at the same time."

I couldn't help but smile, because I had been thinking the exact same thing. Maybe one day it could actually happen.

But for now, I wanted to focus on taking care of my man. "What are you doing home?" I asked with a playful grin.

"I thought I'd come home for a lunchtime quickie," he replied with a mischievous glint in his eye.

We both laughed, knowing that what we just did was far from a "quickie." But it was definitely satisfying.

"Did you finish?" I asked, without needing to clarify what I meant.

"No, but this was incredible," he answered with a satisfied sigh.

I reached down to wrap my hand around his hard cock. "I want you walking back to work with a spring in your step," I purred and wrapped my lips around him.

Tasting myself on his skin only fueled my arousal even more as I pleasured him with my mouth and hand. It was the perfect end to an already amazing experience.

I can get most of him in my mouth, but his length would gag me every time I let him go too far. I'd been working on this, hoping to eventually deep-throat all of him. I relaxed and took him as far as I could, then dragged my lips back up to the tip of his cock, sucking the whole time. I slid my lips up and down his shaft and used my hands to stroke him at the same time.

His breathing became shallower and punctuated with little grunts and moans, his fingers gripped the comforter, and his legs began to shake—I knew he was close. I kept up the rhythm going but added more pressure to my mouth and hands. A moment later, he groaned, releasing warmth into my mouth.

I kept on sucking him until he cried out, "Okay, enough."

I laughed and then swallowed every drop as he watched. Giggling, I nestled into his side.

23

Ryan shook his head, smiling. "Wow, you seem to have changed while I was on this last deployment."

"I've just been thinking of ways we might enhance our sex life," I replied as he got up and headed to the bathroom to clean up.

"Perhaps we can discuss our ideas later," he said when he came out of the bathroom.

So, he has ideas too? I was curious to hear what they might be.

As he got dressed, I couldn't help but notice his euphoric smile, which made me happy. I hadn't expected any of this when I sent in that order form all those weeks ago. And to think I'd even been scared. Little did I know that it would begin a whole new chapter in our lives.

Chapter 2: The Toy Store

Ginger

One evening, shortly after our first experience with Bob, the kids were safely in the care of a babysitter while we went out for a quiet dinner and a movie. But as we left the theater, instead of turning toward home like I expected, Ryan took a sharp turn out of town.

Curious, I couldn't help but ask, "Where are we going?"

Ryan simply grinned back at me but kept driving. My mind raced with possibilities as we drove for about fifteen minutes until I finally saw a large, familiar sign on the side of the road: Adult Toy Store. I had seen it before while passing through this area but never gave it much thought.

As we got closer, my eyes widened in realization. "Are we going to the adult toy store?"

Ryan's mischievous grin only confirmed my suspicions. "I thought we could add a few more items to your collection."

I couldn't help but roll my eyes at his choice of words—Bob was hardly an item in my inventory. But judging by Ryan's expression, that might soon change.

"Let's park on the side of the building," I suggested nervously as he pulled into the parking lot. Call me paranoid, but I didn't want anyone to recognize our car if they happened to drive by.

We stepped out of the car, and I eagerly reached for Ryan's hand, my heart racing with excitement. We'd never been inside an adult toy store before, and I couldn't wait to explore all it had to offer. From the outside, the building seemed fairly plain and unremarkable, but my imagination was already conjuring up images of dimly lit interiors and questionable characters lurking within.

My hand trembled slightly as Ryan opened the door and pulled me inside. To my amazement and relief, a dazzling array of colors and bright lights immediately greeted us. My eyes darted around in wonder at the vast selection of toys, clothes, movies, and various wooden furniture pieces with straps that reminded me of objects described in some of the steamy books I'd read.

As we wandered through the aisles, I couldn't help but notice there were only three men in the entire store. Perhaps it was just my imagination, but it felt like they were all staring at me.

I giggled nervously as Ryan stopped to examine an entire wall filled with vibrators and dildos in all shapes, sizes, and hues. He plucked one off a hook that looked like it could have been as big as his arm.

"What on earth do you plan to do with that thing?" I blurted out, my jaw dropping in shock.

A mischievous grin spread across his face. "Oh, I think we can find a way to make it work."

Shaking my head in disbelief, I walked away as he chuckled behind me. Maybe this wasn't such a great idea after all. But then my attention was drawn to racks upon racks of brightly colored clothing and lingerie. As I strolled past a handsome man holding a lacy negligee up to himself, I couldn't help but smile.

My feet carried me toward a display of corsets, something I had always admired on women. I knew Ryan would love to see me wearing one, and a purple one with black lace edges was calling my name. The next rack over held a leather skirt that I was certain would look stunning when paired with the corset.

With excitement bubbling in my chest, I slipped into the dressing room and made sure to lock the door behind me before undressing. Just as I was down to my panties, there was a knock on the door. My heart skipped a beat until I heard Ryan's voice.

"Ginger? Is that you?" he called out.

Trying my best to conceal my half-naked state, I replied, "Yes, it's me. Just give me a minute."

I could hear him chuckling in amusement. "No problem, take your time."

The corset hugged my waist, cinching in just enough to give me an hourglass figure. Though it wasn't as tight as I preferred, the black fabric still accentuated my curves perfectly. With a satisfying click, I unlocked the dressing room door and stepped out onto the brightly lit sales floor.

Ryan's eyes immediately fixated on me, his features twisting into a lustful grin. My heart fluttered with anticipation. This was exactly the reaction I had hoped for.

He strode toward me, his hands reaching for my hips as his hungry gaze trailed down to my exposed cleavage.

"Damn, this looks hot," he murmured, tracing his fingers over the tight fabric of the corset. "This is definitely going on our initial purchase list." He let out a low growl, and before he could lower his mouth to my breasts, I playfully lifted his chin and laughed.

"What about you?" I asked teasingly, nodding toward his own outfit.

He brushed off the question with a dismissive wave of his hand. "I'm already perfect."

I coughed out a loud laugh, then leaned up to kiss him, savoring the electric tingle that ran through my body at his touch. Eventually, we broke apart, and I retreated back into the dressing room to change back into my own clothes.

When I emerged once again, Ryan was waiting for me with a purple vibrator in hand. The shaft was clear and visibly longer than Bob (our current toy of choice), with small beads nestled inside. A rubber extension on one side resembled the forked tongue of a snake.

My cheeks flushed as Ryan held it up to show me. "What about this one?"

I quickly examined what it was, and how it worked, while scanning the store to make sure no one was watching us. Despite feeling completely comfortable with Ryan, I couldn't help but feel self-conscious in an adult toy store.

After some consideration, I replied, "Okay, I think I'd like that one."

Ryan's grin widened. "Perfect. Let's grab the clothes and this new addition to our collection. And maybe we can pick up that magazine on the counter for more ideas."

I followed him to the cashier, who rang up the clothes and vibrator. She opened the package with nimble fingers, revealing a sleek blue device nestled inside. The cashier's eyes sparkled mischievously as she explained, "We usually put the batteries in to make sure it works before the customer leaves the store."

My cheeks flushed with embarrassment as her words sank in. I watched in fascination as she deftly inserted the batteries and turned on the device. A low hum filled the air as she cycled through all the functions, demonstrating how the beads rotated inside while the entire vibrator bended and swirled. The thought of experiencing such pleasure made an involuntary smile spread across my face, though I tried to hide it.

The cashier turned to us with a knowing look. "Would you like me to keep the batteries in?"

Before Ryan could even shake his head no, I blurted out eagerly, "Yes!"

Ryan raised an eyebrow at my enthusiasm but didn't object as he paid for our purchase. The cashier handed us our discreet little bag with a wink. "Enjoy!"

As we made our way back to the car, I was lost in anticipation and hardly noticed anything around me.

On the drive home, Ryan pulled out onto the freeway. It was late and dark, with only a few scattered cars

29

on the road. Without hesitation, I reached into the bag and pulled out the vibrator.

"What are you doing?" Ryan asked with a mixture of amusement and surprise.

Ignoring his question, I giggled as I slipped off my heels and then wiggled out of my pants and panties. Leaning back against my seat, I spread my legs wide and glanced over at Ryan, who couldn't resist stealing glances at my exposed state. "Keep your eyes on the road," I quipped playfully.

My heart raced as I pushed the vibrator inside, feeling the intense vibrations against my sensitive clit. My body tensed up as waves of pleasure washed over me, making me bite my lip and press my head back against the seat.

I was lost in the sensation, not caring if Ryan drove us off the road as long as that wonderful vibrator stayed inside of me. Its internal vibrations and swirling beads hit all the right spots, sending me into a frenzy of ecstasy. My mind drifted into a hazy state of pure pleasure, completely lost in the moment.

"Breathe!" Ryan called out.

I didn't know how long I'd been holding my breath, but my consciousness gradually returned. I pulled the vibrator out of me, feeling a rush of satisfaction as I placed it back in its package.

Once I was dressed again, I couldn't help but giggle at the naughtiness of what had just transpired in the car. Ryan, who had been watching with amazement while still keeping us safely on the road, looked at me with a mischievous grin.

"I can't wait to use that on you when we get home," he said with a hint of excitement in his voice. "I think Bob might have some competition for your affections."

Laughing at the thought of two vibrators vying for my attention, I eagerly anticipated what awaited us in the bedroom.

We finally arrived home, and Ryan drove the babysitter back to her house while I headed upstairs to get ready for bed. I carefully hung up my new, alluring clothes in the closet and eagerly pulled out the new toy. As I sat on the edge of the bed, running my fingers over its smooth surface, I couldn't help but wonder about the mysterious world of adult stores and the people who frequented them.

Ryan and I had always joked about visiting one together, but it wasn't until now that we actually took the plunge. And as I lay there on the bed, naked, with the vibrator by my side, I realized how naive we'd been to let rumors and stereotypes keep us from exploring our sexuality in new and exciting ways.

Suddenly, I heard the front door open and close, followed by footsteps running up the stairs. My heart raced with anticipation as I watched Ryan enter the room with a grin on his face. He wasted no time in shedding his clothes, leaving them scattered around the room as he climbed onto the bed.

With eager hands, he grabbed the vibrator and positioned himself between my legs. His eyes were like those of a child on Christmas morning, full of excitement and curiosity. And I was more than happy to be his present.

As he pressed the vibrator against my entrance, my body tensed in anticipation of its buzzing vibrations. But to our dismay, nothing happened when he pressed the buttons. Confusion clouded his face as he tried again and again to make it work.

Sitting up beside him, I took control and pressed all the buttons just as I had done in the car earlier. The beads inside began to rotate, but still no vibration.

Ryan's eyebrows furrowed in frustration. "Did you break it on the way home? How hard did you push that thing?"

I couldn't help but laugh, my cheeks flushed with embarrassment. "I couldn't have broken it," I protested.

But no matter how hard we tried to fix it, the vibrator remained stubbornly silent.

Ryan paused for a moment, the childish glint in his eyes turning into a devilish grin. "Just for that, you're getting it all, baby," he said, his voice tinged with excitement.

Feeling a mixture of alarm and anticipation, I laughed nervously. "Umm. What do you mean by 'all?' "

He chuckled and told me to slide down to the middle of the bed and lay back. My heart raced as he reached into my nightstand and retrieved Bob, our trusty vibrator.

With a mischievous sparkle in his eye, Ryan positioned himself above my mouth. "Okay, baby, make those pretty lips of yours do magic, and no matter what I do, don't bite." He lowered himself down, pulling my thighs open.

"Don't do anything crazy, and I won't bite," I said as I took him in my mouth.

Meanwhile, my mind was trying to pay attention to his actions below. He pulled my legs back, locking them behind his arms. He slid his tongue through my center and then over my ass. A moment later, I felt something cool and wet being rubbed on my ass before his finger slipped inside me. Confusion turned to surprise as I realized he'd lubed up for anal play. While I'd never been a fan of it in the past, the last time Ryan used Bob on me in this way had been surprisingly pleasurable. And now, seeing his eagerness to explore this new territory only added to my arousal.

My focus remained on giving him pleasure with my mouth while I tried to relax my muscles for what was about to come. But then something larger worked its way into my ass. Was it Bob?

No, the rotating beads created a unique and pleasurable sensation inside me. In that moment, I was thankful that the vibration feature wasn't turned on, because the combination of sensations would have been too much to handle all at once.

But as Ryan's attention shifted from my mouth to my body, I couldn't help but moan in pleasure and anticipation for what was to come next.

As soon as Bob came to life, I knew exactly where this was headed. My body trembled with anticipation as

Ryan's fingers slid between my folds, spreading my natural lubrication and preparing me for what was to come. With every touch, my body became more sensitized, ready for the pleasure that was about to consume me.

The feeling of fullness that overcame me when Bob entered me was indescribable. Every inch of my body quivered and pulsed with desire. The two toys pressed against the wall between my ass and pussy, sending waves of ecstasy through every nerve ending in my body. The vibrations of Bob's motor only intensified the swirling beads inside me, and vice versa. It was a symphony of stimulation, driving me closer and closer to the edge.

My mind struggled to focus on the sensation of Ryan's cock in my mouth, but it was becoming increasingly difficult as his thrusts grew more aggressive. I moaned around him as fire and fullness consumed me. I completely gave myself over to the moment. With one cock in my mouth, and another in my ass, and one in my pussy at the same time, there was no room for anything else in my mind.

I couldn't help but wonder what we must look like to an outsider—a woman being pleasured by three men simultaneously. The thought alone was enough to send sparks flying through my body, igniting a volcanic explosion from deep within me.

My hips moved of their own accord, meeting Ryan's thrusts with equal force as our bodies moved in perfect synchronicity. The orgasm hit me like a tidal wave, shaking me from the inside out and crashing over me again and again. I couldn't keep track of time, or space, or anything other than the sensations coursing through my body.

I could feel myself reaching my limit and gasped out, "That's enough!"

With great effort, I managed to stop Ryan, and he removed the toys from my body, laying them aside. My chest heaved as I struggled to catch my breath. But before I could fully recover, Ryan was back between my legs with a hunger in his eyes that made my face flush even hotter than before. With determination in his gaze, he positioned himself between my legs and pushed them wide open, exposing me completely. And I loved every moment of it.

Without hesitation, he entered me with a force and intensity that reignited all those nerve endings inside of me. No need for a slow buildup this time—just pure, raw passion driving us both toward an explosive climax.

I couldn't keep my legs up by my ears any longer, every muscle in my body straining as he relentlessly drove into me. "Oh yes, fuck me, Ryan. Fuck me hard."

His body tensed and his breathing quickened, signaling that he was about to climax. I was close too, my own building with each thrust.

With a deep growl, he pressed deeply into me, and I could feel the pulsating as he reached his peak. It pushed me over the edge, and I cried out in ecstasy.

But our moment of passion was interrupted by a sudden voice from the doorway. "What's going on? You woke me up."

Shit. One of the kids!

Ryan rolled over quickly, pulling the covers over us as we scrambled to cover ourselves. Our son stood there, rubbing his eyes, looking confused at the scene before him.

"What are you doing out of bed?" Ryan snapped, trying to regain control of the situation.

"I heard noises in here, and I couldn't sleep." Our son stood there, still not quite grasping what was happening.

I looked at Ryan and placed a calming hand on his chest. "I'll put him back to bed." I sat up, holding the blanket around me. "Go back to your room, and I'll be right there to tuck you in."

As soon as he left, I couldn't help but burst out laughing. "Well, that'll teach you to lock the door."

Ryan laughed too, shaking his head at the unexpected interruption. I got up to tuck our son back into bed before returning to our room.

Picking up the vibrators from where they'd fallen on the floor, I took them to the bathroom to wash them off before bringing them back to our nightstand. As I walked back, I let my robe fall to the floor, enjoying the way Ryan's gaze lingered on my naked body.

Snuggling up next to him, I couldn't help but comment, "Well, that certainly made for an interesting end to the night."

He looked at me with a smirk. "It sure did. Although I may have pulled out before I was finished."

We gazed down at the tangled and rumpled comforter, now adorned with glistening evidence of our passionate lovemaking.

"Don't worry," I reassured him with a grin. "It's laundry day tomorrow." Quickly grabbing a towel, I wiped up as much of the dampness as possible.

A feline smile appeared in his eyes as he lay back on the pillows, his hands resting behind his head. He stared up at the ceiling, lost in thought.

"You know," he commented casually, "that was almost like you having a small gang bang."

I laughed, knowing he was just teasing me. "Is that something you want to watch? Multiple men having their way with me?"

His smug grin only grew wider. "Maybe," he replied slyly.

#

That experience opened up a whole new world for Ryan and me. We began to frequent adult toy stores, discovering a plethora of exciting and daring items to experiment with. Vibrating cock rings, restraints for wrists and ankles, and blindfolds all became part of our growing collection. Gone were our previous reservations about who went to places like that. We were now proud members of that community.

The thrill of trying out new things in the bedroom with the person I loved was exhilarating. We indulged in different types of vibrators, flavored lubes, and even remote-controlled eggs. A word of caution: If you decide to

37

insert a remote egg before heading out for an evening, and give your husband the control, be prepared for some unexpected surprises. You may find yourself blushing as your insides vibrate uncontrollably while your husband looks on with a childish grin on his face. It may be slightly embarrassing . . . but also undeniably cute.

Chapter 3: Introduction to Swinging

Ginger

Nineteen years of marriage had passed, and we were now approaching our forties. Like any long-term relationship, we had our fair share of ups and downs, but through it all, two things remained constant: our deep love for each other, and the unbreakable bond of best friends. Our physical connection was equally strong, as we indulged in sex nearly every day, or at least every other day, when Ryan wasn't deployed. We relished in exploring new sexual adventures together, pushing boundaries and growing more comfortable with each other over time.

After a wild night at Ryan's high school reunion, we found ourselves in the back of his truck, ready to sleep off the alcohol, when I impulsively threw my panties at him and dared him to take me on the tailgate. He eagerly obliged, fueling the fire with the added thrill of potentially getting caught. Another memorable encounter took place at a bar, where we role-played as strangers, sending subtle signals to each other while trying not to tip off the clueless bartender.

But our spontaneity didn't just stop in public places. We've taken our passion to the woods, spreading out on a blanket under the stars, indulging in a spontaneous lunch date in the back seat of the car in a random parking lot, and even venturing off-trail at a park, where Ryan pressed me up against a tree.

At home, we would often let our imaginations run wild during sex, sharing fantasies out loud. What if another

39

man, or woman, joined us? These thoughts seemed to excite us both, prompting further discussion and exploration. We'd heard about swinging and key parties but had never delved into the world of polygamy before. So we decided to do some research and see what possibilities awaited us.

Surfing the web, we realized it was everywhere and that it was a lifestyle for many. It was a way people lived their lives, some full-time, others part-time. We read articles and stories and watched a few online videos. We even read about an entire religious following that seemed to be something of a sex cult. We thought that was a little strange . . . but hey, if it made people happy, then why not?

We eagerly searched for a nearby location to explore, but not too close to home in order to maintain our privacy. After some digging, we came across a group near Philadelphia called "the Cove," roughly an hour away from us. Further investigation revealed it was an "off-premise" club, meaning no sexual activities were allowed on the premises. This distinction seemed simple enough. The website provided limited information—mostly rules and a few pictures from past events. As we scrolled through the images, we saw smiling faces, laughter, and dancing, making it seem like any other nightclub experience.

Ryan turned to me with excitement in his eyes. "What do you think? Want to go?"

We'd already explored many new things together: battery-operated toys and semipublic sex with the thrill of potential discovery. But this was different. It wasn't just a shared fantasy in the privacy of our bedroom. It was real people who were looking for real sexual encounters with other couples. Was I ready for that? I took a deep breath.

"I'm willing to check it out. But let's remember, we're only going to observe, and nothing more."

His face lit up as though he'd won the lottery. On the other hand, I couldn't shake off my apprehension.

Chapter 4: The Cove

Ginger

The anticipation of our visit to the Cove made the day seem endless. We spent the morning at the park with the kids, Ryan finding moments to whisper his desires to me with a sly wink. My mind was consumed with thoughts about possible outfits and hairstyles for tonight. I was a bundle of nerves as I prepared for an evening unlike any other we'd experienced before.

But as the afternoon wore on, the stress faded away. Our children were now in their teens, old enough to stay home alone, so we ordered them a pizza and got ready for the night ahead. The club's website recommended we arrive an hour early for an introduction, so we made sure to leave with plenty of time.

Ryan effortlessly dressed in a button-down shirt, slacks, and dress shoes—Why was it always easier for men?—and I chose a sleek black dress paired with strappy black heels. After blow-drying my hair, I stood in front of the mirror, scrutinizing my appearance. Ryan came up behind me and clipped a delicate necklace around my neck, gazing at me through the reflection, and leaned down to kiss my earlobe.

"Tilt your head," he whispered, lips brushing against my skin as he ran his hand along my neck. "We don't have much time."

I giggled and pulled away. "Stay put." Picking up his cologne from the dresser, I sprayed some onto his neck.

"There. Perfect," I said with a quick peck on his lips. "Even if it's just for me."

He wrapped his arms around my waist and pulled me close. "Are you ready?"

I nodded eagerly, and he took my hand in his.

"Let's go see what it's all about."

Before leaving, we went through our usual checklist, reminding the kids not to burn down the house and making sure they had our cell numbers. We hoped they wouldn't have to call us, but it was better to be safe than sorry. Then we were off on the hour-long drive to the Cove.

As we neared our destination, I couldn't help but fidget in my seat, desperately trying not to bite my nails. At one point, I even suggested we just go out for dinner instead. But Ryan simply smiled and placed his hand over mine, gently caressing the back of my hand with his thumb. His reassuring touch and warm smile were all I needed to calm my nerves.

"Remember, we're just checking it out, sweetie," he said.

With a deep breath, I realized how silly I was being. There was nothing wrong with exploring something new together. As we pulled into the parking lot of the Cove, a sense of excitement and adventure washed over me.

Little did I know what the night had in store for us.

As we approached the location, a throng of people crowded in front of the entrance, their laughter and excited chatter filling the air. We drove around the block and finally found a parking lot in the back.

When we stepped out of the car and made our way to the Cove, the organizers greeted us warmly at a table by the entrance and handed us membership documents to sign. After paying the door fee, a gracious hostess led us inside and gave us a tour. The space was expansive, with a large dance floor, booths, and tables scattered throughout.

Ryan couldn't help but ask, "Is this a regular nightclub?"

The hostess chuckled. "Yes, it is. We simply rent it for our private party."

I piped up, wanting to clarify what "off-premise" meant, like it said on the website. "So, there's no nudity or sex here, right?"

She laughed again. "Well, an occasional wardrobe malfunction might happen, but there is strictly no nudity or sex allowed. This is where like-minded people come together to socialize, flirt a little—or a lot—and see if there's a spark. And from there, they may go off together to a house, hotel, or simply go home as a couple."

After pausing for a moment, she turned her head and asked us directly, "You two are brand-new to this world, aren't you?"

Ryan flashed a sheepish grin. "Does it show that much?"

The hostess continued to lead us around the venue. "Everyone starts out as beginners. But you've chosen the perfect event to dip your toes in. There are no expectations

44

here. No overwhelming nudity or open sex. Just meet people and enjoy the electricity."

We eventually made our way to the bar, where another friendly face awaited us. "This is Smitty," the hostess introduced. "He'll take good care of you. And if you have any questions, just ask for me. My name is Lisa."

I turned to Ryan and placed my hand on his. "Baby, I need a rum and coke."

Ryan looked up to Smitty, who smirked and asked, "Will that be two rum and cokes?"

"Yes, with a little extra rum for her," Ryan quipped, winking at me.

As more people arrived, we noticed they all looked just like us—same type of attire, same hairstyles, same everything. These were swingers? We hung back by the bar and observed, unsure of what to expect. Despite my strong rum and coke in hand, nerves danced in my stomach. After thirty minutes of watching the crowd, I turned to Ryan.

"I don't know if I can do this," I whispered nervously.

He gently pulled me close and planted a tender kiss on my temple. His warmth against my body was a comforting sense of protection and reassurance that everything would be all right. I was always a worrier, often realizing after the fact that my concerns were unfounded. But in that moment, it was hard to logic myself out of the anxiety. Ryan was used to this side of me and knew how to calm me down.

As we sat at the bar and Smitty served us another round of drinks, an attractive couple approached us and introduced themselves. Hailing from Philadelphia, Paul was a tall, clean-cut dentist dressed in casual business attire, and Holly was a slender realtor with short blonde hair and revealing clothing that left little to the imagination. As they chatted with us about kids and everyday life, they seemed like any other couple we might meet anywhere.

But then their friends arrived, exchanging long hugs and kisses as if they hadn't seen each other in years. Ryan and I shared a knowing smile. We knew what those kinds of kisses felt like after being apart for too long.

We made introductions, and we learned this was our new acquaintances' first event as well.

Holly beamed warmly. "We all started somewhere."

Curious, Ryan asked how long the two couples had known each other. To our surprise, they revealed it had been five years. I suddenly felt like I was walking on eggshells, not wanting to ask anything too personal or potentially offensive.

"You've slept with each other's spouses for five years?" Ryan blurted out in shock. I slapped his arm and blushed in embarrassment.

The group laughed off his comment, with the woman playfully wrapping her arm around her partner's shoulders. "We have some playful times together occasionally," she explained. "Sometimes it's just drinks, a movie, a wine tasting, or a simple barbecue. It's not always about the sex, but more about the excitement of knowing we can, and have, slept with each other's spouses. It brings us closer."

Holly added, "It's a lifestyle that few understand, yet many are quick to criticize."

With a warm farewell, they excused themselves and wished us a great night. As they walked away, I couldn't help my intrigue and slight envy of the trust and freedom within their relationships.

But Ryan and I were just getting started on our journey together.

Smitty smoothly slid us another drink, and we made our way to a cozy booth, where we could observe the scene unfolding before us. The club now teemed with a hundred couples of all races, shapes, and sizes. Each one radiated an effortless comfort in their surroundings, embracing friends with warm hugs and passionate kisses.

But as I sat there, a wave of unease grew within me. The energy in this place was palpable, charged with unbridled desire and anticipation. And it seemed like everyone already knew each other, triggering feelings of isolation and fear within me. What if this night turned out to be more than what we were promised?

As we summoned the waitress for another round of drinks, and the dance music began, we shed all inhibitions like clothes discarded on the floor. Women twirled and gyrated on the dance floor, many of them losing their tops in the process. My cheeks flushed at the thought of dancing topless in front of so many strangers. But upon closer inspection, I noticed they were wearing tiny pasties over their nipples—just enough coverage to technically stay within the rules.

We took in all the socializing and flirting around us. Some women even started making out with each other as their male partners watched with rapt attention. While I'd never been attracted to women, there was something undeniably sensual and intimate about their lips connecting. Their touch was softer, gentler. And as my thigh brushed against the front of his body, I could feel his arousal growing. When I looked up at him, our eyes met and he blushed, embarrassed by his own desires.

"Hey, we're only human," he joked, trying to lighten the mood. And with a laugh, I couldn't help but agree. I, too, had been checking out the other men in the club, even imagining a few of them taking Bob's place.

As the night wore on, the air pulsated sexual energy, drinks and dances blurring together. But when Ryan embraced me and finally asked if we could go home, I let out a sigh of relief. We grabbed our coats and made our way to the door, where he went to fetch the car for us. His chivalry made me wonder if he was hoping for a nightcap once we got home. And truth be told, I felt quite worked up myself.

As we drove home, we debriefed about the event, the people we'd met, and the conversations we had. We were particularly intrigued by the two couples who'd been friends for five years and enjoyed both platonic companionship and sexual exploration with each other.

But amid all the nearly topless women in pasties, intimate displays between women, and spouses swapping partners, a concern crept into my mind.

What if we get jealous?

I voiced my worry aloud. It seemed natural to feel jealousy in such a situation. Would one of us feel inadequate? Or, perhaps, desire someone else more?

Ryan's response was reassuring. "After so many years together, there's no one else in the world who I want to be married to," he said as we pulled into our driveway. "This was just a little extra spice in our lives." He turned off the car and squeezed my knee playfully, mischief dancing in his eyes. "And don't forget how much you like fantasizing about two men. I know that doesn't mean you don't want me anymore."

He was right. Even the thought of it had my body humming with arousal. While I wasn't sure about another woman, I definitely craved the sensations of another man. And as long as we discovered this world together, I knew everything would be all right.

Our bodies could barely contain the electric buzz as we climbed the stairs. The night had stirred something inside us both, and it all came to a head in a passionate frenzy between the sheets.

Afterward, as we lay tangled together, my mind lingered on the topic of jealousy. So, I mustered up the courage to ask, "Do you really think you wouldn't feel any jealousy if we were with other people? What about focusing on whoever we're with?"

His brows furrowed as he considered. "I can't say for sure how I would react, but I don't believe jealousy would be my main concern. My biggest fear is not being able to perform," he admitted.

I couldn't help but laugh at his unexpected response. "Well, maybe you should stock up on some little blue pills, just in case."

We chuckled together before drifting off into a peaceful slumber in each other's arms.

\#

For the next few weeks, the excitement and novelty of swinging took a back seat to our everyday lives. We still indulged in using toys from our special stash under the bed, but that was the extent of it.

However, Ryan brought up the idea to add another man to our intimate activities. It was a tantalizing thought that grew in my mind.

One night, after a particularly passionate lovemaking session, Ryan broached the subject of attending the Cove's monthly social event once again.

I took a moment to consider his offer. The nerves had overshadowed the actual experience. It had been intimidating at first, but looking back, it wasn't as bad as I thought it would be. "Okay, let's go," I said. I leaned in for a kiss and whispered, "Thank you for giving me time to think, and for not pressuring me into anything."

Chapter 5: The Cove, Take 2

Ryan

On a cool Saturday night, Ginger descended the stairs dressed in a sleek coat and her strappy black heels, adding a touch of sexiness to her outfit. A delicate silver braided necklace adorned her neck, and she'd styled her hair into long, wavy curls that cascaded around her face, with the sides pulled back to reveal a pair of stunning hoop earrings. An aura of confidence and happiness surrounded her, igniting my excitement for the evening ahead.

She caught me staring at her, and a mischievous grin spread across her lips.

"What's with the grin?" I asked.

"I have no idea what you're talking about," she replied playfully with a small giggle.

As we drove to our destination, we discussed our expectations for the night: We would simply socialize and get to know other couples. Ginger mentioned feeling more comfortable this time but reminded me not to push her into anything.

Upon arriving, we were warmly greeted by Lisa again.

"Welcome back! You didn't get scared off last time, so that's great!" she exclaimed.

We laughed, and I joked, "Did we pass the first test?"

They joined in our laughter, and Lisa responded, "You did pass. You're back, aren't you? Enjoy your night."

After paying our fee, we made our way inside. This time, there was no need to arrive early, so many couples were already mingling at the bar. We headed toward the coat check, and I helped Ginger out of hers. My eyes widened in amazement at what she wore underneath. A stunning black dress hugged her curves, and the chill of the night made it clear she was not wearing a bra. She smirked at my shocked expression.

"I can let loose once in a while," she quipped. "Now stick your tongue back in your mouth and get me a drink."

I gently placed my hand at the small of her back and guided her through the crowded bar to a spot at the counter. The air was thick with the scent of alcohol and jasmine.

We ordered our drinks, and as I gazed at Ginger's stunning face, she finally caught me staring and asked with a playful smile, "What?"

I chuckled and shook my head. "What happened between last month and tonight?"

She shrugged nonchalantly. "I've had time to realize that the last social wasn't nearly as intimidating as I'd thought it would be, so I'm feeling more relaxed tonight. But don't expect anything too scandalous. We're just here to learn and spend time together." She leaned up and planted a kiss on my lips.

As we waited for Smitty to mix our drinks, we scanned the room. There were already clusters of people socializing with one another, laughing, kissing, and touching.

I turned to Ginger with a grin. "Look how everyone seems at ease."

She simply smiled.

Smitty handed us our drinks, and we mingled with the other guests. We met a few couples and discussed topics similar to last time—professions, children, trips—but no one seemed to be talking about sex. It almost seemed like an afterthought. Weren't we all here for that reason? It started to seem otherwise.

As the evening progressed, and the DJ began playing music, the atmosphere in the club became electric. All around us, people danced, kissed, and engaged in passionate lip-lock sessions. Most of the action was initiated by the women, while the men respectfully followed their lead. And what a lead it was. My heart raced and my body tingled with anticipation. The DJ's music changed to a faster beat, and the dance floor filled up even more. Ginger and I had always loved dancing together, so we glided through the crowd, taking in all the sights.

Eventually, we moved to a secluded corner of the room, where only a few other people were nearby. Ginger took my hand and guided it through her cleavage, pressing it against her breast and the hardness of her erect nipple. I gasped in surprise, feeling like I was experiencing this for the first time all over again. Though I'd touched her breasts countless times before, this moment was exhilarating.

As she pressed my hand against her chest, I eagerly grabbed on like a teenage boy trying to sneak a feel at prom. My eyes darted around nervously, wondering if anyone else could see us, while feeling a rush of excitement at the thought of being a "bad boy."

"See, I can be fun," Ginger laughed, holding onto my hand as we swayed to the music.

We felt alive and carefree.

When midnight rolled around, we decided to end our evening. I went to retrieve our coats, then helped Ginger into hers. I turned her around and kissed her deeply. Gazing into her stunning blue eyes, I whispered, "I love you, baby. I'll get the car."

Once I pulled the car up to the entrance, Ginger slid gracefully into the passenger seat. She held out her hand, placing something black and lacy—her panties—into my palm. Shocked and speechless, I just stared at it as she let out a playful giggle.

"Drive," she said with a mischievous smirk on her lips.

As we left the bustling city behind, Ginger unfastened her seat belt and gracefully slipped out of her coat.

"What are you up to?" I asked with a playful grin.

Ginger responded with a sly smirk. "Just something . . . spontaneous." With a mischievous glint in her eye, she kneeled on her seat and leaned over to unzip my pants.

"Focus on driving," she whispered as she pulled me out of my pants and stroked it. Every so often, she'd glance at me with an impish smile before lowering her head into my lap. The sensation of her warm mouth enclosing around my length was electrifying. She alternated between gentle, teasing sucks and quick flicks of her tongue that had me gripping the steering wheel for dear life. It was a challenge to keep my eyes on the road, as all I could think about was the pleasure coursing through my body.

She released me from her mouth and continued to stroke me with one hand as she propped herself up on the seat. "So, which of those other women could you imagine sucking on your cock?" she asked playfully.

I chuckled, trying not to let her words distract me from driving. "Is this some kind of trap?"

She laughed and shook her head. "No way. I genuinely want to know."

I named a few women who we'd talked to at the party, one of whom Ginger had mentioned being attracted to.

Ginger shifted in her seat, spreading her legs, and lifting up her dress to reveal her glistening sex. My focus wavered, as I couldn't resist reaching over and tracing my fingers along her folds. She let out a soft moan and tilted her hips toward my touch.

"So . . . if one of those other women were sitting here like this, what would you do?" she whispered.

My eyes darted between the road and her inviting body. The temptation was strong, but I managed to keep my eyes on the road as I slipped my fingers inside her. She leaned back with a gasp, rocking against my hand as I used my other hand to stay on the road.

"Can you imagine fingering me and another woman at the same time?" she asked, her voice low and sultry.

I couldn't help but steal glances at her as she looked at me with a devilish grin. I focused all of my pent-up energy into my fingers, driving them deeper inside her and rubbing her clit faster. Her moans grew louder and more urgent until she finally arched her back in a powerful orgasm.

She laughed breathlessly as she took my fingers into her mouth, sucking them clean of her sweet nectar. My arousal only intensified at the sight of her pleasure, and I could barely concentrate on the road.

As we continued down the interstate, Ginger repositioned herself back on her knees and leaned over my lap. A mischievous spark danced in her eyes as she sucked on me with expert precision, despite the fact that I was going seventy miles an hour down the highway. Her soft lips and skilled tongue ignited a fire within me. I could barely focus on the road as she teased me with her mouth, whispering seductive words in between each lick and suck. My mind filled with wild images of her, and other women, lavishing their attention on me at the same time, and my balls tightened in response.

"Can you imagine me and another woman sucking on your cock at the same time?" Ginger asked with a wicked grin.

The mental image alone pushed me over the edge, and I couldn't hold back any longer. "Oh my God, here I come!" I cried out as I exploded into her mouth. She continued to suckle me with fervor. The dashboard became a blur as each wave of pleasure pulsated through my shaft.

Breathless and overwhelmed, I randomly shifted my attention from the road to Ginger as she sat back in her seat with a satisfied smile on her face. She dramatically displayed the struggle to swallow the volume down, making me speechless.

She laughed, breaking the tension. "Wow, that was a lot, and it didn't take long. I guess those thoughts really excited you," she said, buckling her seatbelt.

Still trying to process what had just happened, I stole glances at her every few seconds. "Who are you?" I finally managed to blurt out.

We both burst into hysterical laughter.

When we arrived home, we were both exhausted from our wild encounter in the car. But it was a night we would never forget. Ginger thanked me for not being pushy, and for letting her take things at her own pace. Little did she know, that small show in the car had more than convinced me of her true desires. As we cuddled in bed, I couldn't help but wonder, *Who is this enchanting woman next to me?*

Chapter 6: Our Final Move

Ginger

As the year passed, Ryan received orders to move. His assignment was not one of his top choices, but it would be his final duty in the military. After dedicating fifteen years to serving his country and enduring countless deployments around the world, we both craved stability for ourselves and our children. This move would mark the end of his military career, and we could finally consider where we wanted to spend our retirement from the military in five years.

Our family packed up our belongings and settled into an upscale lake community near Charleston, South Carolina. The transition went smoothly, as we were no strangers to moving. Our new home had views of the serene lake from every angle, and a canal in our backyard. Once our children enrolled in school, we had some time to catch our breath.

I had taken on a part-time job as an accountant, with flexible hours so I could make the most of my days while the kids were at school. It had been well over a year since we'd last discussed swinging, and just like before, Bob was involved in reigniting our interest.

Together, we decided to explore swingers' social websites for any local events we could attend. We found several websites, but Swing Lifestyle, or SLS, seemed like the best fit for us. Hesitant to put ourselves on a website like this, especially with our pictures, we proceeded with caution.

First we set up our profile and chose our location. We decided to use a nearby zip code instead of our actual one. In our introduction, we briefly described who we were and that we were interested in connecting with men, women, and other couples. We also made it clear that this was our first foray into the lifestyle. As for our profile picture, we chose one where our faces were blurred out. It turned out, many others on the website did the same thing.

Once we were set up on SLS, we eagerly searched through profile after profile. Within just twenty-four hours, our inbox overflowed with messages from single men, followed by even more the next day. Though we weren't opposed to single men, the overwhelming number of messages featuring shirtless poses, exposed genitals, and fish-holding shots made us quickly decide to turn off that portion of our search. We wanted something more meaningful.

It became clear that everyone seemed to be seeking "drama-free" encounters. It made us wonder just how much drama was involved in this lifestyle. We had yet to encounter any drama ourselves when we ventured out to the Cove. However, what caught our attention were the numerous blanked-out faces in profile pictures— understandable for discretion purposes.

We couldn't help but feel intrigued by some of the more erotic and alluring poses displayed in certain profiles, which caught our eye. But as we clicked on each profile, we noticed significant physical differences between their various pictures, making it difficult to determine which one was current. Most of them only featured a picture of the wife, though I personally found myself more interested in exploring with men.

We came across common acronyms like DDF and DTF. Curious about their meanings, we looked them up online and discovered that DDF stood for Drug and Disease Free, which was definitely something we hoped for in potential partners. DTF meant Down to Fuck, leaving no room for ambiguity about what some couples were looking for.

After carefully choosing a few profiles that piqued our interest, we sent out direct messages, hoping to make connections. However, days went by without a single response. Were these people even real? Was SLS just another fake website? We decided to add more details about our interests to our profile and removed the fact that we were new and just exploring. And it seemed to do the trick. Soon enough, we were chatting with multiple couples. After a few months of virtually getting to know various couples, Ryan and I finally decided to take the plunge and meet one in person.

Chapter 7: Our First Date

Ryan

After weeks of searching for the perfect couple, we finally set up a meeting with Pete and Carrie. We admired their attractive faces and fit bodies in their photos. Our date was set for a Friday evening, which gave us a few days of anxious waiting.

When Friday arrived, Ginger spent two hours getting ready with palpable excitement. As we were about to leave, I realized we didn't have Pete and Carrie's phone number to confirm our meeting. I quickly sent them a message, hoping they'd respond in time. After a few tense minutes, we received an email from them, informing us they couldn't make it after all. Frustrated and disappointed, we wondered why they couldn't have let us know earlier. What would have happened if we'd shown up at the time we agreed?

Despite the letdown, Ginger was still dolled up and determined to make the most of our evening. We went out and enjoyed each other's company over a glass of wine and a discussion about our shared love for the Cove. We wondered if there was something similar near our new home. However, we couldn't help but feel annoyed by the flakiness of this couple.

Deciding to put them on hold until they reached out to us again, we turned our attention to other potential couples who'd messaged us. Some only contacted us once before they disappeared, while others asked about our level of experience before also going silent.

61

However, Jim and Terri stood out as a fun couple, who engaged in lively conversations with us through our messages. They shared their attractive photos and requested ours in return, which we learned how to upload privately to avoid anyone else discovering us. Jim's profile described him as five foot eleven with a muscular build and salt-and-pepper hair framing his handsome face. Terri stood at five foot six with a toned figure and blonde hair cascading down her back.

After numerous emails back and forth, Jim and Terri suggested meeting at a local bar for drinks on Saturday evening, giving us only three days to prepare. This time, we made sure to exchange phone numbers in case of any last-minute changes. To our relief, they were more than happy to oblige.

On Saturday, Ginger asked me if I'd heard from our potential friends. Time seemed to drag until I finally texted Jim to confirm our plans for the evening. His prompt reply, filled with enthusiasm, reassured us that everything was still on track. With a renewed sense of excitement, we gazed once again at their photos, feeling increasingly intrigued.

As we got ready for the night, our daughter curiously wandered into the room and inquired about our plans.

Ginger replied with a sly grin, "We're going on a date tonight, and I want to look my best for your father."

Our daughter shook her head in amusement before walking away.

To ease any nerves, we decided to arrive early and enjoy a drink together before meeting Jim and Terri. As we entered the restaurant, the warm evening air enveloped us. We chose a table outside, where we could people-watch while waiting for our friends. The restaurant was fairly empty, allowing us to easily spot the familiar couple making their way toward us.

Ginger and I exchanged a knowing glance. "Is that Jim and Terri?" I questioned.

We did our best to recall their online photos, but other than some characteristics like their hair and faces, they didn't quite match up. Despite this discrepancy, we greeted them warmly as the hostess seated them at our table.

As we shook hands and exchanged introductions, we noticed Jim was significantly heavier than his pictures suggested, with more strands of gray hair peeking out from beneath his baseball cap. Terri also appeared larger than her stated weight of 120 pounds, with noticeably larger breasts compared to her online profile. Nonetheless, they were both still attractive. We ordered drinks as soon as they sat down, and exchanged polite small talk.

Ginger and I shared another silent exchange of looks about how different Jim and Terri were from their profile photos. While we may not have been the spitting image of Ken and Barbie ourselves, there was no denying that we looked much closer to our online representations. This was certainly an unexpected turn of events, but we resolved to make the best of it.

As we sat and talked, our conversation uncovered that we and the other couple had limited swinging experience. We shared stories about our families, careers, and travels, but apparently, their adventure résumé was just as sparse as ours. Despite this, they were kind and easy to talk to, though not quite what we had anticipated.

Finally, with some hesitation, I asked the nagging question: "How often do most people update their profile pictures? We just added new ones a few days ago."

Jim chuckled. "Our pictures might be a bit outdated, but our profiles accurately represent who we are. Plus, we've made some wonderful friends through this site, so we never felt the need to update."

I replied with a light tone, "We weren't scared off. We just didn't recognize you at first." But I could tell by their exchanged glances that they sensed otherwise.

After an hour or so of conversation, we decided to end the evening on a positive note. We politely shook hands and gave hugs before parting ways.

However, on the ride home, Ginger couldn't contain her frustration and disappointment any longer. "What the hell was that?"

I laughed lightly. "Either they were lying, or we just have bad luck."

We were both disappointed. If we'd met them randomly, we may have been more drawn to them, but our expectations had been set and then let down. We hadn't planned on taking things all the way with them that night, but we were open to it if everything clicked. Ultimately, it was Ginger's decision whether or not to pursue things further with them, but the message was clear—it wasn't going to happen. We spent the rest of our drive home in silence, and when we got back to our place, we went through our usual presleep routine.

As we lay in bed together, Ginger broke the silence. "We need to screen these people better. I guess we still don't know how to find the right matches."

I couldn't help but chuckle. "You looked at their profile too, dear."

She laughed, and we cuddled closer. "I guess we still don't know how to find the right matches."

As the next week arrived, we eagerly perused more profiles, scrutinizing each one to determine whether their pictures were truly current. After much searching, we found another couple who piqued our interest, and we decided to send them an introduction message. We engaged in online chats with them and sensed a fun connection in our exchanges. Excited for what could possibly be our first successful match, we set up a date night for the following Saturday.

But as fate would have it, this couple also couldn't make it at the last minute. This time, at least they had the courtesy to inform us earlier in the day.

Undeterred, we decided to try one more date for the following week. Once again, we chatted online with another couple and got to know them before asking about the validity of their profile pictures. To our relief, they confirmed their pictures were, indeed, recent. The couple's names were Pete and Susan. Susan, with her short brown hair and striking figure, posed provocatively with her hands cupping her breasts in her profile picture, which I found incredibly arousing. Pete had graying brown hair, a strong build, and a well-groomed beard and mustache. Though Ginger was uncertain about his appearance from his picture alone, their charming personalities shone through in our email exchanges. We agreed to meet at a local restaurant.

Arriving early once again to calm our nerves as we waited, my excitement grew when Pete and Susan walked in. They looked just as they did in their profile pictures, except this time, Susan's breasts were covered by her blouse, not her hands.

As we settled into our seats and conversed, it became clear that we all got along quite well. Laughter filled the air as we shared drinks and appetizers, but I couldn't help but notice that Ginger seemed disinterested. On the other hand, Susan was incredibly attractive and clearly showing interest in me. With every flirtatious comment, my arousal spiked, and I shifted uncomfortably in my seat. Though Ginger remained engaged in the conversation, I couldn't help but wonder if something was wrong. Had someone said something offensive? Was she feeling unwell?

About thirty minutes into our date, Susan excused herself to use the restroom and invited Ginger to join her. As they walked away, Pete turned to me and suggested, "If you're both up for it, we can pay the tab and continue the evening with more drinks at our house. Who knows where things might go from there?"

Eager for any opportunity to move this evening forward, I replied, "I'd love that, but let's make sure Ginger is comfortable with it as well."

When Ginger and Susan returned, I noticed a newfound ease in Ginger's demeanor and a subtle smile directed at me. Perhaps they'd coordinated their plans for the rest of the evening. The anticipation grew as we finished our wine and I signaled for the waitress to bring us the check.

As we said our goodbyes, Susan chimed in, "We had such a lovely time tonight and would love to see you again soon."

My mind raced with excitement at the thought of our future encounters with this couple, especially since Susan looked incredibly desirable. It was truly a night filled with potential and intrigue ahead.

I reeled with confusion and disappointment. I couldn't understand what had gone wrong. The evening had seemed to be going perfectly, so why weren't we heading back to their home, or a hotel room? As the four of us walked toward the parking garage, I tried to push away my frustration by replaying the events of the night in my mind. Had I said something wrong?

We all exchanged affectionate kisses as we said goodbye to each other's spouses. My lips lingered on Susan's, and our tongues danced together in a teasing embrace. But as my hand reached up to tangle in her hair, she pulled back with a deep inhaling smile and whispered, "Perhaps we can continue this another time."

My very first kiss with another woman was electrifying, and it left me wanting more.

Ginger and I said our goodbyes to Pete and Susan and made our way back to our car in silence. Once inside, I took a deep breath and finally mustered the courage to ask her the burning question: "What happened?"

"He stared right through me!" Ginger's words cut through the tension between us.

I scowled at her, feeling defensive. "Of course he did. He wanted to get down your pants!" There's something to be said about replying too hastily without thinking.

As soon as the words left my mouth, I regretted them. Ginger's next words hit me like a slap in the face: "Take me home."

As we drove, guilt flooded over me as I realized how inconsiderate and selfish I had been. "I'm sorry, baby," I apologized sincerely. "That was uncalled for. Let's talk it through. What do you mean he stared right through you?"

Ginger struggled to find the right words to describe her discomfort. Finally, she managed to say, "Susan noticed I was uncomfortable, which is why she invited me to the restroom. She asked if something was wrong, and I told her that it was our second date with another couple, and I wasn't sure how I felt."

Susan understood immediately, and gracefully took the lead in ending the evening on a positive note. They'd probably been expecting more from us, but they handled the situation with maturity and kindness. It was a valuable lesson for us on how to respectfully handle unexpected situations.

We then realized how difficult it was to get started in this lifestyle. How did those couples at the Cove get along so well together, have so many laughs, build their connection? What were we doing wrong? We arrived at home and, well, let's just say we didn't make love that evening.

Ginger asked that we put any further dating on hold for a while.

Chapter 8: Our First Hotel Social Event

Ginger

Our once-bustling life gradually slowed down over the next several months. With our two sons grown and starting their own journeys, we now just had our teenage daughter to keep us company for a few more years. In an attempt to revive some of the excitement from our earlier days, Ryan and I resumed chatting with other couples online. However, at this point, we had no plans to actually meet up with anyone in person.

One day, while browsing through a popular lifestyle website, we stumbled upon an advertisement for a social event at a local hotel. The description boasted a dance floor, food, and a cash bar. It also mentioned an after-hours party. We clicked on another tab to see who else had signed up for the event and were surprised to find that we didn't recognize any names. It seemed like none of the couples we'd met thus far were attending.

Ryan and I discussed it, and we ultimately decided to attend the social portion of the event but skip the after-hours party. It would be nice to have a night out dancing, similar to our previous experiences at the Cove. So, we signed up and made sure to communicate our expectations for the evening beforehand. In this lifestyle, clear communication between partners was crucial and set the foundation for a successful relationship.

As the day of the party approached, we couldn't help but notice that the list of attendees had nearly doubled in size in just a couple of days. Suddenly, the event seemed more daunting and nerve-racking. But after talking it over, Ryan and I reminded ourselves that we were only going to socialize and dance. Nothing more. We reassured each other that this would be similar to the Cove, which felt like ages ago now. And, most importantly, we reminded ourselves that communication was key as we navigated this lifestyle together as a couple.

Ryan

On the night of the social, Ginger spent hours in front of the mirror, painstakingly perfecting every detail of her appearance. When she finally made her grand entrance downstairs, I couldn't help but stare in awe. She was a vision in a stunning red dress that highlighted her piercing steel-blue eyes and accentuated her alluring cleavage. The way her nipples pressed against the fabric revealed that, once again, she had forgone a bra. As my gaze trailed down her body, I suddenly felt her hand on my chin, tilting my head up to meet her eyes.

"Hey, my eyes are up here," she playfully scolded.

We both laughed, and I couldn't help but express my admiration for her beauty. Her long, wavy hair cascaded down her back and perfectly complemented her flawless makeup. The new black strappy heels with metal details showcased the toned curves of her calves, leaving no doubt that she was dressed for success tonight—success measured by the number of admiring gazes she would surely receive.

As for me, I opted for the standard "guy wear" of khaki slacks, a black button-down shirt, and polished black dress shoes.

71

Ginger sniffed at my neck and gave me a coy look of disappointment. I quickly took the hint and dashed back upstairs to spritz on my neck the cologne she loves so much.

With our daughter, Abby, safely settled in with her friend for a sleepover, and pizza ordered for their dinner, we were ready to embark on our evening.

The hotel that was hosting the social was not exactly high-end, but we were surprised to see how many cars were already parked outside. As we made our way toward the entrance, we merged with a sea of incredibly attractive people. Some were dressed in jaw-dropping outfits that left little to the imagination. One woman caught our attention with her fishnet dress, revealing faintly visible strings of her panties underneath. She proudly flaunted her lack of a bra, opting instead for pasties that matched the color of her dress. As if that wasn't bold enough, she wore a necklace with the words "Fuck Me" hanging in gold letters.

Another brunette woman caught our eye in a stunning floor-length evening gown. Her back was completely bare, down to the top of her shapely derriere. A small section of fabric covered her midsection before opening up on both sides down to her ankles. The slit in the dress exposed most of her thigh with every step. It was clear that she'd strategically placed double-sided tape to keep her breasts from spilling out. Despite the daring outfit, she looked absolutely gorgeous. Upon closer inspection, we noticed her earrings were small replicas of male genitalia, adding a playful touch to her overall look, and setting the tone for the wild evening ahead.

The hotel lobby had all the typical trappings, but there were also some scandalously dressed people mingling about. We followed the crowd through a makeshift wall made of black plastic and found ourselves in a hallway adorned with streamers, balloons, and even a table full of sex toys and genital-shaped candies for sale. It was clear that this was not going to be just any ordinary night out.

As we made our way to the registration table, I couldn't help but notice how many of the guests seemed to already know each other. It reminded me of our first party at the Cove. We approached the table, where one man and three women sat, checking names, taking money, and handing out wristbands. Despite our initial excitement, we soon realized there was not only a forty-dollar fee for the event, but also an additional annual membership fee of forty dollars. My disappointment was evident as I handed over the cash.

Ginger leaned in close to my ear. "Think of it as a prepayment for getting laid tonight."

I chuckled and looked at her with a smirk. "I've never had to pay for it before."

"You pay for it all the time. You just don't realize it," she teased back. We shared a laugh before paying and signing waivers. As we turned to leave, a stunning blonde woman caught my attention with her revealing dress and ample cleavage. She took our money with a smile, and then gestured beside me, reminding me that Ginger was waiting for me.

Busted. My guilty leer quickly shifted from the woman back to Ginger, who stood beside me with her hands on her hips and head tilted to one side. We both laughed before moving on to get our wristbands.

As we entered the ballroom, it appeared like any other hotel ballroom with white linen tables decorated with flickering candles, and lounge chairs scattered in the middle. But there were also balloons across the large dance floor with a stage set up at one end. Making our way to the closest cash bar, I ordered our drinks.

Just as we took our first sips, an energetic couple approached us. "Ryan and Ginger?" they asked with excitement.

We hadn't been expecting to see anyone we knew here, so we were caught off guard. The couple seemed nice enough, but they appeared twenty years older than us. He sported dockers, a polo shirt, and deck shoes while she wore a short black dress that showed off her petite figure and black hair. Her gray eyes sparkled under the lights and captivated me instantly.

"Hi," I said, extending my hand to shake his.

Our first encounter with a couple left us feeling embarrassed and disoriented. Despite their friendly smiles, Ginger's eyes widened in confusion as she looked at me for some sort of recognition. But it was clear—we had no idea who these people were.

"Sorry," I said, hoping not to offend them. "We've chatted with a few couples on SLS. Could you remind us of your names?"

"No worries," the man replied, chuckling. "It can be hard to keep track of everyone. We're Eric and Sandy.

We've exchanged messages a couple of times and recognized your pictures."

Only those whom we were interested in getting to know better had access to our face pictures. As they spoke, my mind raced, trying to recall this couple. We continued the conversation politely, but I couldn't shake the feeling that something was off. They seemed much older than us and didn't quite match any of the online pictures I could remember. Eventually, we excused ourselves and headed toward the hotel's hors d'oeuvres table.

The aromatic scents of cheeses, crackers, fruit, chicken wings, ribs, shrimp, and various salads overwhelmed my senses. Our initial confusion was quickly replaced by hunger as we each grabbed a plate filled with delicious food. With our plates in hand, we made our way back to the ballroom, where we sat down at a table to eat and observe the other guests around us.

Ginger pulled up her phone to browse through Eric and Sandy's profile. But as soon as we saw their pictures, it became clear—there was almost no resemblance between them and the couple who stood before us. How long ago were these pictures taken? And did everyone on the website use old or misleading photos? The thought lingered in my mind as we indulged in the mouthwatering spread of food before us.

As we walked through the bustling crowd, a couple approached us and introduced themselves as Ben and Liz. They had an air of confidence and sophistication, with well-kept appearances that suggested they had a few more years under their belts than us.

Ginger and I exchanged a glance, wondering if this was another case of mistaken identity. "Did we happen to chat online this past week?" I asked, hoping to clear up any confusion.

Ben chuckled, leaning in as if sharing a secret. "I don't know, did we?"

We all laughed at the absurdity of the situation. "Actually," I admitted, "this is our first SLS event. We chatted with a few couples beforehand, but it's hard to match profiles with faces."

Ben nodded knowingly. "Ah yes, that's common. Some people use older or more flattering pictures in their profile to attract attention, and then rely on their personality when meeting in person."

Ginger and I exchanged a skeptical look. This was not what we expected from a swingers event.

"It's true," Ben continued. "Of course physical attraction plays a role, but what's most important is finding laid-back, drama-free individuals. That's always been our focus."

I couldn't help but ask, "Why do so many profiles mention 'drama-free?' Is there really that much drama in the lifestyle?"

Ben paused for a moment before answering thoughtfully. "Think back to high school and dating. Sometimes those immature behaviors resurface in some people within the lifestyle. Not everyone, but it does happen."

76

Despite our initial reservations about Ben and Liz, we found ourselves enjoying their company and learning more about the reality of this lifestyle.

"What exactly happens upstairs after this part of the party ends?" Ginger asked curiously.

"We actually have a room up there for the night," Ben explained. "After eleven, this group moves to a secure floor, where there will be more food, drinks, and a much wilder time. Nudity and sex are not uncommon."

I could feel Ginger tense up next to me at the mention of nudity and sex. We both knew this was something we were interested in exploring, but it was still new territory for us.

"Do you plan on going up there, since you paid for the entire night?" Ben asked, catching on to our hesitation.

I looked at Ginger, silently pleading for her input. She didn't give me any indication, but I didn't want to make a rash decision and potentially ruin our first experience in the lifestyle. "Not this time," I finally answered. "We have to get home early tonight."

Ben handed us an SLS meeting card with their names, website screen name, and phone number. We stared at it in awe. It almost felt like a business exchange. Were they professional swingers?

"It's just a free service offered on the SLS site," Ben explained. "Feel free to contact us with any questions. We've been around the block a few times, and if we don't know something, we definitely know someone who does."

The lively dance music pulsed through the crowded room, beckoning everyone to move with its infectious beat. Ginger excused herself to use the restroom, and I took the opportunity to observe the dynamics of the people on the dance floor. It reminded me of the Cove, with women dancing provocatively and men reveling in their company. My attention was drawn to two couples dancing together. Their movements were fluid and intimate as they exchanged kisses and caresses with each other.

Ginger returned with a mischievous grin on her face and placed something small and lacy in my hand. "Here, hold these for me tonight," she said, her eyes glinting with excitement.

My thumb traced over the delicate lace fabric, sending a thrill through my body. She knew how much it aroused me. Suddenly, she grabbed my head and pulled me into a passionate kiss before dragging me onto the dance floor.

As we swayed to the music, I discreetly tucked her panties into my pocket. She leaned in close to my ear, her lips brushing against my skin as she whispered, "If you can do so without anyone noticing, you can feel how wet I am."

I raised an eyebrow in surprise but didn't back down from her challenge. We danced closer to a group of people, and I slipped my hand through the slit in her dress and between her legs. My fingers found their way to her arousal, causing her to gasp and lock eyes with me.

"Okay, that's enough," she said breathlessly, motioning toward another couple who'd noticed our actions. We both blushed but couldn't help laughing at our boldness before sharing a quick kiss.

As the night wore on, I couldn't resist sliding my hand over Ginger's breast. Even through the fabric of her top, I could feel the hardening of her nipple, a clear indication that she was just as turned on as I was. We had come a long way from our first visit to this club.

As the clock approached 11:00 p.m., the majority of people had left the ballroom area. A voice came over the speakers, thanking everyone for attending and announcing that the after-party was about to begin.

We made our way out of the ballroom, ready to head home, when we were stopped by the man who had put wristbands on us earlier.

"Aren't you two going to take advantage of what's happening upstairs?" he asked with a sly grin.

I shook my head. "No, this is our first time here, and we wanted to take things slow."

He nodded with understanding. "I see. Well, then let me introduce myself properly. I'm Cliff, and my wife is Cindy. She's getting ready for the second part of the evening. How has your experience been so far?"

In response, I pulled out Ginger's crumpled panties from my pocket, much to her embarrassment.

Cliff chuckled and raised his eyebrows. "Very nice. Listen, my wife and I are hosting a small party at a friend's house next weekend. It's more low-key than this event, but it's still a lot of fun. We'd love to have you two join us if you're interested."

79

Ginger and I exchanged glances and nodded eagerly. He gave us his profile name on SLS to contact him for more details.

On the drive home, we couldn't stop laughing and holding hands, still buzzing with excitement from the dynamic energy and eroticism of the night. It all translated into another passionate round of sex once we finally made it home.

The next morning, we lay in bed, cuddled up to each other while we discussed our thoughts and desires. Ginger expressed her satisfaction with the atmosphere of these events, but when I brought up the idea of potentially exploring a threesome with another man, she blushed.

"It's definitely something I want to try," she admitted. "But how do we even go about it? It seems so complicated just trying to set up a date."

This was the ultimate challenge. How do we take that first step when the couples we meet never quite live up to their profiles, have dull personalities, or are simply not compatible?

Chapter 9: The Creepy Basement

Ginger

After exchanging a few emails with Cliff and Cindy on SLS, we were intrigued by their fun personalities and the details they shared about their upcoming party. They described it as casual and requested that we bring an appetizer to share. Not knowing what to expect, we approached the event with open minds, figuring it couldn't be any worse than the disappointing dates we'd had so far.

Throughout the week leading up to the party, Ryan and I discussed our fantasies in more depth, becoming increasingly open to the idea of fulfilling our desires. We talked about potentially having two men for me and two women for Ryan, or even just one additional person to get started.

As Saturday finally arrived, we got ready for the party in simple yet stylish outfits of jeans and nice shirts.

Before leaving, I reached into my nightstand and retrieved some condoms I'd purchased a while back and had stashed away just in case. I handed them to Ryan with a smile. "Here, take a couple just in case we connect with someone."

Ryan chuckled as he tucked them into his back pocket. "Just like high school. When were you going to tell me about these?"

"When I felt there was a need, but now you know," I replied with a mischievous grin.

We set off down some winding country roads, driving for over an hour before arriving at the secluded house where the party was taking place. The mailbox out front was shaped like a race car, marking the entrance of a long driveway that led to a well-hidden home nestled among trees. As we pulled in next to another parked car, Ryan and I exchanged excited glances.

"Did you see that mailbox?" I asked with a grin.

Ryan nodded, already smiling from ear to ear. We made our way to the house, noticing two porches—one in the front, where the lawn was patchy and teeming with moles; and one in the back, which was closer to the parking area. We opted for the latter and made our way up the porch stairs. Ryan rang the doorbell, and we eagerly awaited a warm welcome from our hosts.

Cindy was a mysterious figure to us, having only seen pictures of her without having met her at the hotel party the week prior. In her photos, she seemed like an attractive thirty-something blonde woman. But as we stood on her doorstep, the woman who answered was clearly in her late fifties, with deep lines etched on her face, likely from a lifetime of smoking. Her complexion was sallow, and her missing top-middle tooth caught our attention immediately. Ryan and I exchanged silent glances, mentally sending each other red flags.

After Ryan explained that Cliff had invited us here for a party, the woman turned and yelled for him. We couldn't help but feel wary as we waited on the porch.

Finally, Cliff arrived at the door with a woman who more closely resembled the pictures in their online profile.

Our hopes for the evening were restored. As we stepped inside and set down our fruit tray, Cliff introduced us to his wife, Cindy. She greeted us warmly, offering hugs and kisses on both cheeks.

"It's so nice to meet you both," Cindy said sweetly. "I'm sorry we didn't get a chance to meet at the hotel party last weekend." She was quite lovely, standing at about five foot six with fiery auburn hair.

"So, are you new to the lifestyle?" Cliff asked.

Ryan and I shared another glance before I responded, "Yes, very new."

Cindy smiled knowingly and said with reassurance, "Well, you've come to the right place. Just a small gathering of friends, no pressure, and all fun people who will make you feel comfortable."

She then introduced us to Addie, who had been the one to answer the door for us.

"Welcome to our little party," Addie greeted us in a raspy voice, her loose breasts gliding inside of her NASCAR T-shirt as she gave us each a tight hug. "Glad you could make it. The food is upstairs, but the real party is down in the basement. My husband, Ron, is down there with a few others. After a couple shots of courage, you'll be ready to join in on the fun. Make yourselves at home."

Slowly, we followed Cliff and Cindy down the creaky stairs. As we descended, Cindy's voice echoed through the dimly lit basement. "Now, the atmosphere here might be a little rough around the edges, but the people are great, and we always have a good time."

The steps felt steeper than usual, almost like descending into a hidden underground lair. Ryan held my hand tightly as I carefully maneuvered sideways to avoid tumbling forward.

Finally, we reached the bottom and took in the cluttered decor of the basement. The space seemed large, but it was filled to the brim with boxes and random items stacked haphazardly—old beer cases, antique racing signs, and other racing memorabilia towered up to the ceiling.

Cindy waved off our bewildered expressions with a laugh. "Oh, don't mind all this stuff. Addie and her husband are NASCAR pack rats who think they'll find their retirement on eBay. Come on, there's an open area over here where we hang out."

Navigating through the maze of boxes and items, I couldn't help but wonder if we'd need to leave breadcrumbs to find our way back out. We passed by piles of old motorcycle parts and stacked tires before we finally reached an open space, where a few people were already socializing.

One man stood up from his chair, and Cindy introduced him as Addie's husband, Ron. He was tall and lanky with long, thinning hair and a full gray beard and mustache. His number 3 hat matched the one on their mailbox outside.

As he leisurely made his way over to us, Ron gave Cindy a quick kiss, and then turned his attention toward us. "Well, well, who do we have here?" he said with a grin.

Cindy simply replied, "This is Ryan and Ginger. They're brand-new around here, so you'd better behave."

Ron shook Ryan's hand, and then leaned in for a hug with me. I tentatively hugged him back, keeping my eyes on Ryan the whole time. I was starting to have second thoughts about coming to this party.

Ron then introduced us to the rest of the group, who were gathered in their makeshift hangout area. Cindy and Cliff soon excused themselves to help Addie with something upstairs, leaving us alone with the others.

There were two sofas covered with sheets, a few chairs scattered around them—also covered with sheets, and a coffee table made from an old wooden door resting on top of two tires. I held onto Ryan's hand tightly, using my grip as a way to convey that I wasn't entirely comfortable being there.

But Ron nudged us toward one of the sofas. "Have a seat, join the party."

As we settled onto the plush sofa, Ryan quickly retrieved drinks from the cooler and joined me in a facade of comfort in a strange basement with people we didn't know.

Across from us sat two other couples, their bodies angled toward each other in conversation. We struck up a lively discussion with them, learning that one of the couples had also attended last week's hotel party. Despite racking my brain, I couldn't recall seeing them being there among the crowd. It had been a blur of people, most of whom I wouldn't be able to recognize if I saw them again.

Curiosity got the best of us, and we asked how the party had progressed throughout the night.

The husband eagerly recounted, "It was a sea of lingerie and sleepwear, with some rooms featuring exhibitionists putting on a show for others to watch. Plenty of kissing and oral activity going on. All in all, it was quite an experience."

We chatted and laughed with the couples, while Ron silently listened with an amused expression. As we talked, I couldn't help but scan the room for possible escape routes. The piles of junk surrounding us gave off an eerie feeling. If anything were to happen to us down here, we would surely never be found.

Suddenly, Ron grabbed his Dale Earnhardt coffee mug and casually mentioned, "Oh, by the way, the bathroom is located over there near the washing machine. Just remember to jiggle the handle after flushing."

We thanked him with smiles before returning to our conversation. But as time passed and more drinks were consumed, we couldn't help but notice when another couple entered the basement. They were young and attractive, likely in their early twenties.

Ron stood up excitedly and exclaimed, "There's my sugar! Come here to Daddy!"

Ryan and I exchanged glances as the girl made her way over to Ron and locked lips with him in a passionate kiss. His hands roamed freely over her body before settling on her backside, eliciting a playful squeal and giggle from her. Our suspicions were confirmed—they were into the whole daddy-and-little-girl role-play. While it wasn't our cup of tea, we didn't judge.

Ron then pulled in the young man for a hug, pretending to punch him in the stomach before bursting into laughter. "Damn, boy, how many times did you tap that pretty little thing this week?"

The young man playfully blocked his side and replied with a laugh, "I lost count."

The girl joined in on the laughter, teasingly adding, "There's still plenty of me to go around."

We couldn't help but grin at the jovial attitude of Ron and his companions. Ron, with one arm around each of them, turned to us and said, "For some of you who are new, this may seem a little awkward, but I'd like to introduce you to my son, Billy, and his wife, Kate."

I felt Ryan's eyes on me as my mouth dropped open in surprise. Now I was judging. I was judging hard. I desperately wished for Ryan to read the get-me-the-fuck-out-of-here message that I was sending through my eyes.

Billy and Kate greeted the other couples around us with obvious familiarity. They walked around and introduced themselves to us before sitting down next to us on the sofa. Ryan sat stiffly next to Kate while Billy casually placed his hand on my leg.

"Are you two the newbies who Maw told us about? We were new about a year ago, but ever since Maw and Pa invited us to a party down here, we've been hooked."

I forced a smile and tried to be polite for several minutes while we made small talk. Meanwhile, I watched Kate's hand run along Ryan's leg, occasionally pausing at his growing third leg. His hand started to glide along her

87

leg, and with her encouragement, it disappeared under her dress.

He was thinking with the wrong head, and it was clear that I needed to remind him of our plan to leave. So, I discreetly reached for his leg closest to me and pinched him with my nails. He snapped his attention back to me, finally understanding my unspoken demand.

Ryan stood up abruptly. "I think we'll go upstairs and get a bite to eat." He grabbed my hand as we hurriedly made our way through the maze of people. They probably saw straight through our excuse, but at that point, I didn't care. No one said a word as we reached the stairs and climbed up to the second floor.

When we got to the kitchen, it was thankfully empty. I smiled, thinking we would finally be able to escape this awkward situation. We headed out to the back porch.

"Is something wrong?" came a voice from behind us.

Shit! Busted! Cindy and Addie were there on the porch, smoking.

"I hope you weren't scared off," Cindy said with a hint of concern in her voice.

Ryan replied nervously, "No, it's just that we're still very new and not quite sure what we're looking for. But thank you so much for your kind invitation."

Addie leaned on the porch railing, a cloud of smoke billowing from her exhale as she silently observed us. Cindy responded with a friendly smile, "Well, we hope to see you again soon. Have a safe drive home."

"Thanks!" I said with forced enthusiasm as we quickly made our way across the porch and down the stairs. I didn't dare look back as we got into our car and drove away, relieved to have escaped without causing any further discomfort or suspicion.

The silence in the car was thick and heavy as we drove away. My mind was swirling with thoughts, emotions, and questions that I couldn't hold back any longer.

"What the hell was that? Is that what house parties are like?" I practically spat out the words, still trying to process everything we'd just witnessed.

Ryan's laughter only fueled my frustration. I smacked his arm hard.

"It's not funny. Did you see their son there, with their daughter-in-law? And they have sex with each other! They have sex with their own children!" The disgust and disbelief in my voice was palpable.

But Ryan just smiled and reached over to place his hand on my leg. "Relax, baby. Breathe."

I smacked his arm again, feeling a surge of anger at his nonchalant reaction. "And what the fuck was with you sliding your hand up her dress, knowing I wanted to leave? You've been inconsiderate in the past, but this topped it all!" I glared.

"I'm sorry, baby. She was very pretty, and she actually pulled my hand up her leg." His excuse only angered me further. "You're right, sweetie," he continued, trying to defuse the tension. "I'll be more considerate in the future."

I let out a frustrated sigh and leaned back against my seat, still reeling from the events of the afternoon. This was not at all what we'd expected. Despite trying to calm down, I couldn't help but feel on edge as we passed endless trees on the interstate.

After a while, I turned to Ryan again. "I need a break from this. We need to find someone sane, and I'm not going to another house party unless we really know the people first."

Ryan nodded understandingly and placed his hand on my leg again, this time in a comforting gesture. "Yes, dear, I completely agree."

I shook my head, still trying to process how anyone could engage in the kind of activities we'd just witnessed.

The rest of the car ride was spent in tense silence as I stared out the window, wondering if this lifestyle was really for us. It seemed impossible to find a couple we were actually interested in without encountering a disturbing or unsettling situation. Maybe Cliff and Cindy could have been that couple, but their connection to strange and questionable activities made me hesitant. Would we ever find a couple who truly fit with us in this lifestyle? Only time would tell.

Chapter 10: Our Awakening

Ryan

Months passed with the lifestyle pushed to the back burner. Ginger and I found ourselves able to go on dates again after years of focusing on parenting. It was a feeling we'd both missed for over two decades. Occasionally, we would log into SLS just to see if anything new had popped up, or if we had any messages, but otherwise, normal life consumed us, and neither of us felt a desire to partake in the lifestyle.

But one night, Ginger and I decided to try something different and check out a local bar called the Hitching Post to see a live band. We'd never been there before, as we'd heard rumors that their regular crowd was rough and rowdy. However, we were intrigued by the fact that an eighties cover band was playing, and we both enjoyed dancing, so we figured it was worth giving it a shot.

Spontaneity took over, and we didn't have time to change into anything fancy. We were simply dressed in jeans and nice tops. We paid the cover charge at the door and were directed to sit wherever we pleased.

As soon as we entered the bar, we couldn't help but take in its . . . unique appearance. It seemed like a cross between a biker bar and an Old West saloon. The dance floor in front of the stage was made of polished wood, while the long bar on the right side of the building was adorned with Western and biker decorations. Booths lined the other three walls, and wooden tables scattered the floor like a restaurant. There weren't many people inside, but most of

91

those sitting at the bar—clad in Harley Davidson attire with hardened expressions—were not the type of people we would typically come across in our daily lives.

We made our way toward a booth opposite to the bar, trying our best to ignore a sour smell that hung in the air—a mixture of motor oil and mildew. However, it was hard to ignore the attempted artwork carved into most of the tables we passed by—clearly the work of bored men with pocketknives.

As we settled into a booth, we saw another couple sitting a few seats away, who seemed to be around the same age as us and dressed similarly. So, perhaps we weren't completely out of our element after all.

We ordered some drinks and an appetizer, engaging among ourselves in conversation about our children and how we now only had one left living at home. We talked about what we would do once we were empty nesters, realizing all we knew how to do was raise a family. We then both realized we couldn't remember the last time we'd gone on a spontaneous date—perhaps a year ago. This led us down memory lane, reminiscing about our teenage years and the dates we'd been on: The straw loft in the barn, walking down to the creek with a blanket, slipping off the trail at a state park for a quick romp, and even the time Ginger's father had caught us playing strip poker with friends before we got married. As we laughed and talked, ate and drank, it felt like I was courting my wife all over again.

As the pulsating beat of a Pat Benatar tune filled the room, we were drawn to dance on the wooden floor like moths to a flame. Despite the crowd gathered at the bar and around the tables, only one other couple swayed in unison on the floor—the pair that were nestled in the nearby booth. The woman yelled over the music, her voice laced with playful sarcasm, "Looks like no one else appreciates this kind of music!"

We chuckled, glancing toward the bar, where curious eyes watched our spontaneous display of enthusiasm. We continued moving to the rhythm, soaking up every moment of joy and freedom.

When the band took a break, we made our way back to our booth. The other couple introduced themselves as Jack and Deedee, claiming to be locals who frequented this place for its great live performances. Jack stood shorter than me with a sturdy build, broad shoulders, short hair, and a neatly trimmed mustache. His infectious smile never seemed to fade, and his words brimmed with positivity. Deedee was petite with auburn hair and a dazzling smile that could light up any room. Simply being in their presence made it difficult not to feel happy.

We exchanged stories and small talk while standing near their booth. Eventually, Deedee asked, "Would you two care to join us?"

Ginger and I shared a mischievous look before she gave a nonchalant shrug. "Sure," I replied with a grin.

We settled in next to our new friends. Jack and I talked about everything from outdoor pursuits, like hunting and fishing, to local news and events happening in the area. I caught snippets of Deedee and Ginger's conversation about parenting, popular hangout spots, and Deedee's dance lessons, and it became clear that we all had plenty in common.

As Billy Joel made his grand entrance onto the stage, the four of us made our way back to the dance floor. The music was even better than before, and we all moved as a tight-knit group, since no one else seemed eager to join in on the fun. Ginger and I twirled and laughed, relishing every moment of this unexpected night out. We were truly having the time of our lives.

The band took a much-needed break, and we retreated to our cozy booth. Jack, always the life of the party, suggested a friendship shot, and we all agreed—well, Ginger agreed on my behalf, since I was the designated driver for the night.

As Jack and I caught up on old times and discussed his hunting cabin and some prime fishing spots, I couldn't help but steal glances at Ginger and Deedee as they chatted animatedly. They seemed to get along well, but I noticed a subtle change in Ginger's smile. It was no longer genuine but more of a facade, with a hint of anger simmering just beneath the surface. Her eyes kept darting in my direction whenever Deedee was talking, a familiar look that never boded well.

Despite the tension brewing between them, we all made our way back to the dance floor as soon as the band started playing again. Ginger danced a bit farther away from me but still beckoned me over with a curl of her finger, her faux smile still plastered on her face. But as soon as I reached her and moved away from Jack and Deedee, her smile vanished.

"You set this up, didn't you?" she hissed through gritted teeth.

Confused, I furrowed my eyebrows and tried to make sense of what she meant.

"They asked if we were swingers and invited us back to their house," she continued angrily.

My eyes nearly popped out of my head. "What did you tell them?"

"I said I would talk it over with you," she replied.

"I promise I had nothing to do with this," I reassured her, taking her hands and pulling her closer as we danced. "But let's be honest . . . they're definitely more attractive than anyone else we've met. And they're fun to hang out with."

We talked it over as a Bon Jovi tune played in the background. While I hadn't orchestrated it, I couldn't deny feeling a bit excited about the prospect. Deedee was undeniably attractive, and Ginger seemed to think the same of Jack. Plus, we'd been having a great time with them so far.

"It's up to you, baby," I said. "Whatever you decide, I'm okay with it."

"I'm not sure," she replied, biting her bottom lip nervously.

As a song that none of us particularly liked came on, we made our way back to our booth. Deedee wore a knowing smile on her face when we approached. "I take it you two have discussed our invitation?" she asked coyly.

"So . . . are you interested in coming back to our place for some fun?"

My mind was made up, but I turned to Ginger, waiting for her answer. A gradual grin spread across her face, her eyes shining with excitement.

"I'll need another shot!" she exclaimed.

Jack waved down the waitress, and we all chuckled at Ginger's enthusiasm.

She threw back her shot of peppermint schnapps with determination, placing both hands on the table as if bracing herself. Her gaze met mine, and she grinned mischievously. "Okay, let's do it."

After paying our tab, we followed Jack and Deedee out to the parking lot.

"Are you sure about this?" Deedee asked when we reached their car.

Ginger and I exchanged a look.

"Let's go!" Ginger blurted out. "We've always talked about it, so why not now?"

We climbed into our car and trailed behind Jack and Deedee as they led us to their house.

Ginger squeezed my hand tightly. "You know I'm nervous, right?"

I glanced over at her and gave a reassuring smile. "I know, honey. But if at any point you want to leave, just say the word."

Jack and Deedee lived in a beautiful wooded community filled with two-story and split-level homes. As we stepped inside their house, Deedee discussed some rules.

Rules? We'd read about them on profiles before, things that couples had already decided they wouldn't do with others. But we didn't realize it was something you discussed right before having sex.

"We want to make sure you're comfortable since it's your first time," Deedee explained. "Would you prefer separate rooms, or all of us together in one room?"

Ginger and I exchanged another look. We hadn't really talked about that beforehand. I guess we should have. Finally, Ginger spoke up. "If we're going to do this, then let's go all out and be in the same room together."

My heart raced with anticipation at the thought of seeing both Deedee and Ginger naked at the same time.

"Just to be clear, no means no," Deedee added. "If there's ever a point where you're not comfortable, just say so, and we'll stop. We always use protection and have condoms if you don't. And is there anything you guys are not into?"

Anything we're not into? Ginger and I burst into laughter at the question.

"We don't even know what we're into, let alone what we're not into," she replied with a grin. "Just no ass slapping or hair pulling, and I'll be good."

We all shared another laugh before following Jack and Deedee into their bedroom.

Ginger

My heart raced with eagerness and apprehension, my entire body trembling in the presence of this new experience. I couldn't remember the last time I'd been so nervous. Ryan was the only man I'd ever been intimate with, but now here we were, about to embark on a sexual encounter with another couple. Jack, whom I'd just met a few hours ago, stood before me, his hand clasping mine as he led me through their bedroom doorway.

As we entered, Jack guided me to the side of the bed closest to the door, his touch gentle and respectful. Our lips met in a soft kiss, a stark contrast to the passion that ignited between us. His mustache felt foreign against my skin, unlike Ryan's clean-shaven face. But I pushed aside any doubts and surrendered to Jack's embrace.

His kisses grew more passionate, fueling the fire of desire within me. With my eyes closed, I let my body guide my actions, allowing myself to fully succumb to the pleasure coursing through me. In that moment, it didn't matter that this man was not my husband. All that mattered was my intense craving for him.

Jack's hands roamed over my body, expertly caressing and arousing me. He removed my shirt and bra with ease, revealing my bare breasts to him. The cool air made my nipples tighten, but Jack's touch soon warmed them again as he rolled them between his fingers.

I couldn't help but comment on his skill as he effortlessly unhooked my bra. "You've done this before," I quipped playfully as he discarded it to the side.

He chuckled in response. "A few times."

His lips found their way back to mine but soon traveled southward down my neck and onto my chest. My entire body tingled with excitement as his mouth closed around one of my nipples while his hand worked its magic on the other. I moaned and tangled my fingers in his hair, pulling him closer.

But as he nipped at my sensitive flesh, a slight pain shot through me. "Ouch," I whispered, trying to control my reaction. "Not so hard."

He quickly adjusted his actions, and the pleasurable sensations continued to consume me. My hands roamed over his body, desperate for more of him. With each passing moment, the arousal within me grew stronger.

I stole a glance at Ryan and Deedee, who were caught up in their own passionate encounter. Jack took this opportunity to unfasten my pants, and my heart raced faster. This was really happening.

"Are you okay?" he whispered, sensing my nerves.

With a smile and nod, I reassured him that I was ready for more. He slowly removed my pants and panties, leaving me standing before him, completely exposed. Without hesitation, I placed my hands on his shoulders as I stepped out of my panties at my ankles, feeling supported by his strong presence. Jack tossed them aside with my discarded bra as the thrill of this forbidden encounter consumed me.

My entire body gasped as his lips met my thighs, kissing them ever so gently. The sensation sent shivers down my spine and ignited a fire within me. My sex, now at eye level for him, made me impatient for more. With a slight pressure on my leg, he guided me to step one leg to the side, exposing myself to him further. His mesmerizing smile was all it took for me to give in to his every desire.

I parted my legs even wider, eager to feel his touch everywhere. His approving grin made me flush with heat. I ran my fingers through his hair again as he leaned in closer. The instant I felt his lips on me, I gripped his hair tightly, unable to contain the electricity coursing through my body. No one had ever touched that part of me except Ryan.

As he parted me with his tongue, gently slipping inside of my entrance and then back up to my clit, my eyes drifted closed in pure bliss. After a few minutes of his mouth dining on me, Jack gradually stood up. He kissed his way up from my stomach to my breasts, lingering at each peak before moving on to my neck and finally my lips. His hand slid through my hair at the back of my neck, gently stroking my skin with his fingers.

He asked again, "Is everything all right?"

I smiled and nodded, grateful for his concern for my comfort throughout our first experience together. I eagerly kissed him back as he gently laid me down on the bed.

He gently pulled my legs open wide and knelt between them, looking right between my inner thighs with an expression of penetrating hunger in his eyes. As he lowered his mouth to my heat again, Jack looked up at me and held my gaze as he resumed that intimate kiss. To see a man, someone new and different, intensely desire me was intoxicating. I lay my head back and let the sensations wash over me as he flattened his tongue against my folds.

"Are you enjoying this?" Ryan's voice seemed distant, but I sensed he was still nearby.

"Mm-hmm," was all I could whimper as Jack's lips and tongue explored every inch of my sensitive flesh.

He sucked and licked at my clit with just the right amount of pressure, sending waves of pleasure through my body. His fingers slid inside of me, rougher than Ryan's, which only added to the exhilaration. Another moan escaped me when the tip of his fingers brushed a very sensitive spot inside me, and he stayed there while continuing to suck on my clit, prolonging the deep pleasure until my body couldn't take it anymore. I grabbed his head to steady myself, and he looked up at me in surprise.

I smiled. "That spot is very sensitive."

He beamed back proudly.

I slid off the edge of the bed and knelt before him, hastily unfastening his belt and pants, pulling them down. He stepped out of them and kicked them aside. I bit my lower lip as I drank in the sight of him. He was so different from my husband but equally alluring. I was amazed by his cock and balls, which were completely smooth in the middle of his forest of hair. I ran my hands up his legs, feeling every inch of his masculine body while my core ached even more with desire.

As my fingers slid through his thick hair, I leaned in and kissed his thigh before navigating my mouth around to kiss his other thigh. His testicles hung low and were quite large, making my anticipation grow even stronger. I gently fondled them, exploring and teasing before finally turning my attention to his semi-erect cock, just inches from my mouth. Our eyes met again, and the anticipation and need in his gaze only fueled my desire for him even more.

A glistening drop of pre-cum hung from his tip, tempting me to lean in and slowly lick it off. His body trembled and his thighs twitched in response, sending a thrilling jolt of pride and excitement through me. I wanted more.

Jack's shaft may not have been as large as Ryan's, but it didn't matter. I desired him more than I'd imagined. With eager hands, I caressed his cock as my tongue swirled around the sensitive head. He gripped my hair tightly, a clear sign of his pleasure. Drawing on my experience with Ryan, I confidently continued exploring Jack's cock, occasionally meeting his gaze with a mischievous smile.

"I have some fun talents," I purred. "Would you like to see?"

His enthusiastic nod only fueled my confidence. Relaxing into the moment, I took him deep into my mouth and used my throat muscles to glide back and forth along his length. Jack couldn't help but grab my head in the midst of our passionate encounter. Gagging slightly, I pulled away and met his gaze with a proud grin.

He looked down at me with awe written all over his face.

My pride swelled as he gently pushed me back onto the bed. Meanwhile, Ryan stood between Deedee's legs,

102

thrusting into her with a look of unbridled lust. Her body swayed in time with his movements, her eyes closed and mouth open in ecstasy. It was different from the aggressive sex Ryan and I shared—it was softer and more passionate, just like Jack's approach.

Feeling a sense of contentment wash over me, I watched my husband and Deedee find something special in each other that we didn't share. Their chemistry was undeniable.

But Jack quickly regained my full attention by pushing my legs open and stepping closer. My body tingled with anticipation as he teased the tip of his cock through my slick folds. With a gasp, I welcomed him inside, and he filled me completely.

This was the first time anyone other than Ryan had taken me like this.

Leading up to this moment, I'd experienced many mixed emotions, but right now, all I could feel was pure lust and hunger. Desperate for more, I wrapped my legs around Jack's hips and pulled him in deeper, urging his thrusts to become more forceful.

My eyes fluttered shut as I surrendered to the pleasure. That's when I heard Deedee laugh and opened my eyes to find her crawling toward me.

"Can I kiss you?" she asked with a playful grin.

Looking over at Ryan, who I knew would enjoy watching us, I nodded eagerly. Although we'd just met that night, there was something about Deedee that drew me in. She was stunningly beautiful, and I couldn't resist her any longer. As our lips met in a passionate kiss, I relished in the thrill of being filled by Jack while sharing an intimate moment with Deedee.

Her lips were soft and pliant against mine, moving to the rhythm of Jack's thrusts in perfect sync. She paused briefly to whisper something to Ryan, her breath tickling my ear. When she turned back toward me, Ryan entered her from behind. The sensation of being pleasured by two different people at once caused my body to clench in shared pleasure.

I closed my eyes as she resumed kissing me, feeling Jack's thumb circle teasingly around my clit. The euphoria of this experience surpassed all my expectations, and I never wanted it to end. When Deedee pulled away from our kiss again, I opened my eyes to see her nipple tantalizingly close to my mouth.

Ryan's expression was one of pure desire, like a child peering through a window at a candy store. He wanted to see me suck on Deedee's nipple, and in that moment, I wanted it too—if only to please him. I've never been interested in playing with another woman, but in that moment, my inhibitions were thrown out the window, and my body was on fire. The texture of her nipple against my tongue was incredibly soft, inviting me to take more into my mouth.

She leaned down closer, allowing me to envelop her breast completely as I swirled my tongue around and kissed it in the same way I enjoyed having my own breasts caressed. This was the first time I'd ever tasted another woman's flesh, and I wasn't sure if I was doing it solely for

Ryan's satisfaction, or if a part of me genuinely enjoyed the bisexual encounter. But one thing was for certain—in that moment, I knew this experience would be life-changing.

A moan escaped me as Jack continued to drive into me from behind while holding onto my hips with a firm grip. With every thrust, the head of his cock hit against that sensitive spot within me, sending waves building between my legs. I gasped in pleasure as he continued to thrust, making my breasts bounce slightly with each movement. Unable to resist the powerful sensations, I released Deedee's breast from my mouth.

But she didn't seem to mind. In fact, she leaned down to kiss me again before offering her other nipple to my waiting mouth. I eagerly accepted, sucking on her soft, supple flesh with abandon. It must have been a sight for Ryan, because at that moment, his familiar grunt filled the room.

Deedee pulled away from our kiss and whispered in my ear, "I think Ryan just came."

Feeling a sense of satisfaction wash over me, I fiercely pulled Deedee's lips back to mine, my hand threading through her hair. Her softness, coupled with Jack's hard cock inside me and his firm grip on my thighs, caused the fire within me to grow even more intense. Unable to contain myself any longer, I tilted up my hips to meet Jack's next deep thrust. His soft moans and the pressure of his release on my thighs sent me over the edge, my body trembling uncontrollably as I gripped onto Deedee's arm.

As we lay together on the bed, basking in the afterglow of our first encounter together, we caressed each other tenderly, our faces still flushed with passion. It was a moment that would forever be etched in our memories—a moment of pure drunken bliss and ecstasy that brought us all closer together.

Ryan

My eyes lingered on Deedee's curvaceous figure as she guided me around the bed. Anticipation raced through my veins, threatening to burst a vein with every beat of my heart. As she turned and pressed her soft lips against mine, my primal instincts surged to the surface. Our kisses were filled with passion, my lips trailing down her neck, and my teeth grazing along her shoulder as I gripped her firm ass cheeks. Moving up to her ear, I glanced over to the other side of the bed, where Ginger and Jack were locked in a passionate embrace. Surprisingly, Ginger seemed completely at ease.

At last, we were about to embark on this long-awaited adventure. Though I'd worried about jealousy creeping in, everything felt right for now. Deedee removed her top, revealing her small yet alluring breasts. She took my hand and guided it to one of them, placing her own hand over mine to guide me in caressing her.

"Just relax and enjoy," she whispered before kissing me again.

A fierce desire consumed me, and I ravished her body, eagerly discarding the rest of our clothes with frenzied kisses and wandering hands. Deedee matched my

106

enthusiasm with eager touches and hurried kisses. As we parted lips momentarily for me to peel off my polo shirt, I admired her naked form: petite breasts, shapely hips, and a cleanly shaved pussy that made my cock twitch.

As I leaned in for another kiss, she unexpectedly pushed me back onto the bed with a mischievous glint in her eye. Chuckling at her assertiveness, I propped myself up on my elbows to see what she had in store.

Taking hold of my throbbing cock, she drew closer to me while maintaining deep eye contact and sporting an impish grin.

"I think you're going to enjoy this," she purred before licking and sucking on my balls, starting from the base and working her way up.

Holy hell, did I ever enjoy it. Moving up to the head of my cock, she slickly stroked me with one hand while using her mouth to engulf the tip. Locking eyes with me again, she devoured my cock at a fervent pace. Ginger had certainly given great oral pleasure, but Deedee's more aggressive approach was nothing short of mind-blowing.

Turning my head to the side, I saw Ginger lying next to me with Jack's face buried between her thighs. I whispered to her, "Are you enjoying yourself?"

She whimpered in response, "Mhmm," before gasping once again. Clearly, Jack knew what he was doing.

Deedee drove me wild. Her technique was completely different from Ginger's. The way she stroked me with her hand while expertly sucking on my cock, then purposely choking herself before repeating the process sent electric shocks through my body. Ginger could deep-throat me, but this was something Ginger had never done before, and frankly, something I had never experienced.

Deedee sensually licked her lips as she pulled them off me, slowly climbing onto the bed next to me. Her assertiveness once again took me by surprise, but I couldn't deny that I liked it. We switched positions, and Deedee spread her legs wide for my viewing pleasure. My gaze was immediately drawn to her smooth, hairless mound, glistening with anticipation.

As I reached out to touch her, my attention was caught by movement from the side. I turned my head and saw that Jack and Ginger had also switched roles, with Ginger now on her knees and devouring his cock. The sight of her mouth wrapped around his length sent a surge of desire through me. Instead of feeling jealous, it only added to my own lust.

Deedee noticed my distraction and touched my hand. "Everything okay?" she asked.

Feeling slightly embarrassed, I quickly refocused my attention back on Deedee. "Absolutely," I replied.

She smiled and gestured toward herself. "Good, because this pussy isn't going to eat itself."

With a light laugh, she pushed her legs up and open, inviting me to explore her most intimate areas. I leaned down between her thighs, savoring the view of her smooth skin and delicate folds. Deliberately, I kissed along her inner thighs before gliding my tongue over her silky mound. She moaned in pleasure as I traced patterns along her slit.

Stopping at her swollen clit, I gently circled it with my tongue before taking it into my mouth and sucking on it softly. Deedee tangled her fingers in my hair, urging me to continue. As I pleasured her with my tongue, she gave me directions and guidance on what felt best for her—a little more pressure here, faster there . . . It was exhilarating to discover all of the unique ways to pleasure her that were different from Ginger's preferences. I couldn't help but think about all of the other exciting things we had yet to discover.

Deedee whispered, "There's a condom in the nightstand."

I quickly opened the drawer and handed one to her. She unwrapped it with finesse, showcasing her skilled hands as she rolled it down my length. It was the first time someone else had put a condom on me, and the visual alone sent shivers down my spine.

She lay back again and lifted her legs, displaying her toned thighs and smooth skin. My eyes roamed over her body in admiration. Her bare sex glistened in the dim light, inviting and tempting me to touch it. I moved closer, my hardness throbbing with desire as I placed the head at her entrance, teasingly rubbing it up to her clit and then back down.

Her moans were like music to my ears. "Give it to me. Don't hold back," she gasped, her voice filled with need and desire.

I needed no more encouragement. In a swift motion, I plunged inside of her, feeling her walls stretch and envelop my length. The condom hardly detracted from the incredible sensation, only adding a thin layer of protection between us. As I thrust inside of her, our thighs collided in an intense rhythm.

I watched with fascination as I slid in and out of her, a sight that had always turned me on. She reached down and began to rub her clit vigorously, adding another dimension of pleasure to our passionate encounter. This was something Ginger had never done.

As we continued to move together, she begged for more. "Faster! Harder!" she whimpered, each word punctuated by more forceful thrusts.

I willingly obliged, driving into her with all the speed and power I could muster. Her cries grew louder with every thrust. I took control of her legs and pushed them back as I pounded into her relentlessly.

And then she came, crying out in pure ecstasy as her body tensed and shuddered around me. I slowed my pace, savoring the moment as she relaxed with a satisfied sigh.

But my attention was soon drawn away by the sight of Jack fucking Ginger. Her eyes were closed in bliss, her breasts swaying enticingly with each movement. The view was like something out of a dream, and I couldn't believe my luck.

Deedee, who had been lying next to us, suddenly rolled over onto her hands and knees. She leaned over to

Ginger and whispered something in her ear. My heart raced at the thought of what could possibly happen next.

"Can I kiss you?" Deedee asked, her voice low and seductive.

The question stopped me in my tracks. I hadn't expected this turn of events, but the mere thought of it sent shivers down my spine. I watched as Ginger smiled dreamily at me before nodding her consent.

With bated breath, I watched as Deedee leaned down and pressed her lips against my wife's. Their mouths moved together slowly and sensually. I was mesmerized by the sight, completely caught off guard but unable to look away. It was a moment that would forever be etched into my memory, a moment of pure pleasure and unexpected surprises.

Deedee's eyes met mine, her gaze a seductive invitation. "Are you just going to watch, or are you going to fuck me?"

Her words snapped me out of my trace, and I eagerly accepted her invitation.

I thrust into Deedee, lost in a state of euphoria. Jack was behind Ginger, their bodies moving in perfect harmony. Deedee and Ginger were entwined, kissing and exploring each other's bodies, making sounds of pleasure.

Ginger took one of Deedee's nipples into her mouth, her movements relaxed and deliberate as she sucked and licked. I mirrored her rhythm with my hips, unable to tear my eyes away from the erotic scene before me. Ginger locked eyes with me, a devilish smirk on her lips as she continued to tease me with her actions. My mind couldn't decide which was more arousing: watching my wife enjoy another woman's body, or being teased by her knowing glances.

Deedee broke the kiss and moved her other nipple toward Ginger's eager mouth. As they continued to switch between kissing and suckling on each other's breasts, I felt the pressure build within me. My groan echoed through the room as I released, gripping her hips, pushing inside her as deep as possible. I relaxed, but Deedee seemed determined to prolong our pleasure as she moved herself against me.

Deedee soon pulled off me and turned around, lying next to Ginger. I stayed still as she moved against me, admiring the sight of my cock inside her glistening pussy. She moved herself on me while caressing Ginger's breasts.

As we all lay together in a sweaty heap, Deedee suddenly asked, "So, do you think we can be friends?"

We all laughed at the obvious answer. I was left speechless.

"It was better than I expected," Ginger chimed in, causing Jack to puff out his chest with pride.

"Would you do this again?" Deedee asked playfully.

"Absolutely," Ginger replied, the nervousness she'd expressed earlier replaced by joy and satisfaction.

Her response filled me with relief. The four of us spent more time chatting and laughing, learning more about each other and the lifestyle we'd just delved into. But as the clock struck three in the morning, exhaustion took over. We dressed and said our goodbyes before heading back to the car, our minds still reeling from the unforgettable experience we'd just shared.

As we drove home, our hands intertwined, the warm breeze carrying the scent of blooming flowers through the open windows. I glanced over at Ginger, her hair tousled and a mischievous glint in her eyes.

"So, what do you think?" I asked, unable to contain my excitement.

She smiled knowingly. "Well, this night was definitely unexpected. But I still think you had something to do with it."

I laughed and shook my head. "I swear, baby, it was all just a random encounter. I couldn't have planned it if I tried."

There was a moment of silence before Ginger's lips curled into a grin. "I could get used to this once or twice a month."

I nearly swerved off the road in shock. "Once or twice a month? You were terrified before! What changed?"

Ginger chuckled. "Well, my cherry is popped now, and I had a good time."

Pride and excitement swelled within me as I thought back to our steamy encounter with Deedee. "It was amazing, but the most incredible moments were when she started kissing you, and you were sucking on her nipples."

"I just went with it," she confessed with a coy smile. "But don't expect it all the time."

Just being able to witness that experience with Ginger was enough for me.

We arrived home and said our goodnights before quickly falling asleep.

The next morning came early, and Ginger was already sitting on the porch with a cup of coffee, watching the fog roll over the calm water.

"Thinking about last night?" I asked, joining her with my own cup.

"Actually, yes," she admitted with an enthusiastic grin. "I can't believe how nervous I used to be about this kind of thing. It was so much fun."

"The best part was doing it together," I added, taking a sip of my coffee.

Ginger nodded and took another sip, a hint of mischief in her eyes. "But just because I had a little fun with Deedee doesn't mean I'm into girls. I'm strictly dick-ly, but I knew you wanted to see that, so I decided to go with it and give you a treat."

I chuckled and playfully teased, "If you keep bringing it up, I'll start to think you're not telling the truth."

She laughed and swatted my knee. "I just want to make sure we're on the same page."

We discussed the possibility of our kids finding out about our new adventures and how we needed to be careful and discreet. We'd previously agreed to not discuss it in front of them, or leave any evidence around, but now that we'd finally taken the plunge, we were eager to continue our exploration.

The next day, Deedee called Ginger to check on us and let us know she'd had a great time. They both expressed their desire to meet up again. We thanked her for being our first experience and let her know we felt the same way. With our first taste of this exciting lifestyle, we couldn't wait for more thrilling encounters in the future.

Chapter 11: Mixed Company

Ginger

Deedee invited us to join her with some friends and neighbors for a Saturday gathering of beer and blue crabs. The thought of spending a sunny afternoon with good company, delicious food, and maybe even a little flirtation made me eagerly accept. I couldn't wait to tell Ryan.

"She said it's just friends and neighbors, so it won't be a full-on play party," I explained, already anticipating his mischievous thoughts.

He smirked. "Well, how do you flirt with a mixed crowd?"

I playfully rolled my eyes. "Just be charming and respectful. Remember, these are our first lifestyle friends. Don't ruin it."

Ryan nodded.

The next day, I texted Deedee to ask if she needed us to bring anything to the gathering. She replied that we were welcome to simply bring ourselves.

On Saturday, we arrived at their house around noon. Already, there were a few people milling about on the back patio. Some stood around a small TV perched on cinder blocks in one corner, cheering on a baseball game while holding cans of cold beer. Others sat around a table, expertly picking apart steaming-hot crabs.

"Hot crabs coming through!" Jack called out as he carried a large cookie sheet stacked with crabs to the outside table.

We greeted him and exchanged hugs before he went back into the house to fetch another batch of crustaceans.

"Deedee's inside. Go say hi," he directed us with a smile.

As we walked into the house through the garage entrance, Deedee was at the kitchen sink, rinsing out a pot. Seeing her brought back memories of our steamy first encounter at this very house. Her face lit up with delight when she saw us walk in. She quickly dried her hands and enthusiastically hugged and kissed both of us.

"Welcome to our crab picking!" she exclaimed.

A man with long, wavy blond hair and a deep tan leaned against the counter next to her. Deedee introduced him as their longtime friend, Rudy. He stood as tall as Ryan, his lean frame suggesting a life spent on the beach.

"Let's get you guys some beer and introduce you to everyone," Deedee said, leading us toward the garage door. Suddenly, she stopped in her tracks and turned to face us. "Just so we're clear, if anyone asks, we met at the Hitching Post and became friends. I don't want any misunderstandings, because believe me, they will ask."

We nodded before following her into the bustling garage.

She gracefully led us around the room, introducing us to her diverse group of friends and family. Despite meeting them only a week ago and engaging in intimate activities, it felt oddly natural to mingle with their loved ones so soon. The atmosphere was lively and welcoming, as if we were all old friends reuniting after a long time apart. Jack and Deedee seemed to be the perfect blend of friendship and sexual exploration that we'd been craving.

As we made our way around the room, Rudy silently trailed behind us, his presence radiating a mischievous energy. Every time I glimpsed him, he had this knowing smile on his face, like he held a secret that only he and I were privy to. My cheeks flushed with warmth every time our eyes met, not just because of his devilish grin but also because of his captivating appearance. I found myself almost disappointed that this was just a regular party instead of an opportunity to get to know him more intimately.

Deedee must have noticed our subtle exchange of glances, because when we reached a secluded area, she leaned in close and whispered, "Oh, I forgot to mention, Rudy is one of our highly recommended *friends* in the lifestyle." She emphasized the word "friend" with air quotes. Without missing a beat, she suggested, "Why don't you three go grab some crabs and get better acquainted?"

His hidden secret was unveiled. His playful smirk and suggestive wink sent shivers down my spine as my mind raced with possibilities. My face burned with desire as if someone had lit kindling beneath my skin. It reminded me of being back in high school, trying to play it cool and not give away my infatuation with a crush.

So, Ryan, Rudy, and I made our way outside to feast on crabs and sip cold beers while we talked and got to know each other. Rudy had an irresistible, whimsical charm that drew me in with his quick wit and infectious humor. I tried not to reveal too much about my own desires, but the way I found myself touching his arm or laughing at his jokes gave me away. Yet I couldn't resist his magnetic energy and playful demeanor. He was simply irresistible.

A couple of hours passed in laughter, but then we had to leave because we'd promised our daughter that we'd take her to a movie. Rudy and I exchanged phone numbers, and then we found Jack and Deedee to give them hugs and kisses and thank them for inviting us to their party.

While Deedee hugged me, she whispered, "You won't find a better single guy out there." Many thoughts ran through my mind, and all of them involved Rudy and I in a naked entanglement.

Ryan's hand on my arm chased those thoughts away. I turned to give Rudy a goodbye hug as well. I didn't realize how long I hugged him until Ryan cleared his throat. I stepped back to see him, Jack, and Deedee smiling at the blushing teenager I'd become.

As we got into our car and headed out, I tried to pretend I wasn't a quivering mess. After a few minutes, Ryan woke me from my daydream. "You seem quite smitten over Rudy."

My face ignited again, and I tried not to grin too widely. "Maybe."

The embarrassing warmth remained for another several minutes as I pondered what it would be like to be with Rudy.

Ryan asked, "Do your thoughts involve what Rudy would be like in our bedroom?"

I stared out the window without responding, certain my grin and blush had already given me away.

Chapter 12: Spontaneous Guest

Ryan

I had just arrived home from a long day at work when my phone rang. It was Ginger. I answered, and she immediately launched into her question.

"Remember Rudy from Jack and Deedee's party?" she asked.

"Of course," I replied. "The one you were fawning over?"

She let out a playful laugh. "At least I wasn't drooling. Well, not much. But we've been chatting for the past week, and you know how we've talked about having a threesome with another guy? Well, I was wondering if you'd be open to having Rudy join us."

While I wasn't surprised by Ginger's proposition, I was definitely caught off guard by the request. "Um . . . sure, it could be fun. When were you thinking of doing this?"

"Well . . . I kind of told him to meet us at home in thirty minutes," she confessed. "Could you quickly tidy up the bedroom for me?"

I held the phone away from my ear in disbelief. "What? In thirty minutes?"

Ginger didn't immediately respond, leaving an awkward silence as I tried to wrap my head around the situation. I wasn't a fan of surprises, especially ones that involved strangers coming into our home.

"Is everything okay?" she asked, breaking the tension. "We don't have to do this if you're not comfortable." But, of course, she played the guilt card. "I thought this was something you wanted too."

It was true. We had discussed experimenting with another man before, but not with someone we barely knew.

In a moment of weakness, I gave in to her request. "Sure, it'll be fun. See you soon."

Heading upstairs to clean up the bedroom and gather my thoughts, I couldn't help but think back to our conversations about threesomes being inspired by "Bob." I couldn't deny that the idea turned me on, but thirty minutes' notice was hardly enough time to prepare for a new sexual encounter.

As I picked up clothes off the floor and straightened the bed, I couldn't help but wonder why Ginger didn't discuss this with me earlier. Though I wasn't opposed to it, her impulsive decision was another one of her strange surprises. Checking for condoms in the nightstand, doubt crept into my mind. Why did I agree to this so hastily? And . . . did I even have a choice? It seemed like Ginger had already made up her mind and just expected me to go along with it. This was not communication.

As confused and uncertain as I felt, there was still a part of me that was intrigued. So, I decided to see how things played out, trusting my friends' judgment and hoping for the best. After all, I'd enjoyed watching Jack fuck Ginger at that party. Time would tell if this surprise threesome would be just as exhilarating.

The doorbell chimed, interrupting my thoughts. It must have been Rudy. I glanced at the clock on the dresser. He was early, and I wasn't quite ready for him yet. I took a deep breath to calm my nerves before heading downstairs to open the door. Rudy stood in the doorway, dressed casually in blue jeans, an untucked button-down shirt, and flip-flops. His confident demeanor from our crab picking outing seemed to have faded, replaced by a hint of bashfulness.

"I hope Ginger told you she invited me over?" he said hesitantly.

I smiled warmly, trying to exude a welcoming tone. "Hey, Rudy. Of course, come on in."

My mind raced with questions. When would Ginger be here? Was I supposed to just hang out with Rudy until she arrived? Or were we supposed to get naked and wait for her? No, that would be weird.

"Beer?" I offered.

"Sure," he replied gratefully.

I led Rudy into the living room, where we sat down and engaged in small talk about his experience in the lifestyle. We talked about how long he'd been a part of it and some of his experiences with other couples. He shared a few stories, and just as our conversation started to feel comfortable, we heard the garage door open.

Ginger came through the door and set down her briefcase before turning to look at us with an eager grin. I breathed a sigh of relief. Now I wouldn't have to carry the conversation all by myself.

"Where's my beer?" she playfully pouted, her eyes shining with excitement and mischief.

We laughed, and I excused myself to grab three lagers from the garage. When I returned, Ginger was already greeting Rudy with a passionate kiss. My heart skipped a beat. Damn, she wasted no time.

"Umm. Damn, you work fast," I joked, trying to brush off any feelings of jealousy.

Ginger quickly turned around, a hint of guilt in her expression. "Who, me?"

"I think he means me," Rudy chimed in with a mischievous smile.

I chuckled and joined in on the teasing. "I guess I meant the both of you." I handed Ginger and Rudy their beers, raised an eyebrow, and playfully tilted my head. "Perhaps your husband can get one of those hello kisses too?"

She giggled and wrapped her arms around my neck with an eager kiss. I couldn't help but feel a little unsettled. She seemed more excited to see Rudy than to see me, making me question if I was just an afterthought. But I pushed away these thoughts, chalking it up to nerves and inexperience.

I turned to Rudy. "Well, you have the experience here. Do we socialize for a little while first, or . . .?"

Before he could answer, Ginger cut in. "I'm ready."

Rudy's confident grin returned as he placed both hands on Ginger's hips. "Well then, I guess there's no need for socializing."

I'd expected to chat a little before diving in, so I was caught off guard by Ginger's sudden desire. She must really be into Rudy—and who could blame her? He was attractive and charming, that naughty surfer boy who most women would swoon over. But still, I'd never seen her this eager before.

We made our way upstairs to the bedroom, and as we walked, I couldn't help but wonder how much texting they must have done leading up to this moment. Once inside the bedroom, Ginger disappeared into the bathroom without saying a word.

Ginger

As I stood in front of the bathroom mirror, I couldn't hold back my nerves. I'd wanted this for so long, but now that it was actually happening, I couldn't shake off the butterflies. With a deep breath, I took another sip of beer before undressing and admiring the results of my first Brazilian wax. The smoothness and bareness filled me with pride and anticipation.

Little did Ryan know, I'd specifically gotten the wax to surprise him. But as I stepped out of the bathroom and into our bedroom, it seemed like he would be getting more than just a surprise. Both Ryan and Rudy stood by the bed, completely naked and holding their own beers. Their smiles widened as they saw me enter the room, their gazes immediately drawn to my newly waxed area.

125

Ryan's eyes went wide, and his mouth fell open in awe, while Rudy calmly stated, "Nice."

A warm flush spread across my face at their reactions. It was empowering.

"Come over here, sweetie," Ryan said, beckoning me closer. "Let's have some fun."

My heart raced as I walked toward them, imagining all the ways we could pleasure each other. I took another big sip of my beer for courage before placing it on the nightstand, and then, without hesitation, I leaned in and kissed Ryan first. His hand slid to the back of my head, pulling me closer as his other hand rested on my hip. Behind me, Rudy pressed his body against mine, his hands caressing the goose bumps on the small of my back. He kissed my shoulder tenderly, sending jolts of electricity through me as I felt his erection pressing between my ass cheeks.

My breathing quickened and my desire grew stronger. Our kiss deepened as Rudy's hands moved from my back to my breasts, massaging them while gently rolling my nipples between his fingers. Ryan's skilled hands found their way to my bare cleft and slipped inside, sending shockwaves through me.

As our tongues wrestled in lustful desire, I couldn't resist grinding my body into Rudy's erection, making it clear what I wanted. My body moved instinctively, responding to the touch of both men as they ran their hands all over me. The heat between my legs was almost unbearable. I ached to be taken.

Turning around to face Rudy, a surge of desire propelled me toward him as we resumed our passionate make-out session. Our texts over the past week had been steamy, but this was even hotter than I imagined. Rudy's hands returned to my breasts while Ryan pleasured me with his fingers, his erection now between my cheeks. I reached down to hold both firm pieces of oak, slowly sliding my hands along them, far from coordinated as I struggled to pay attention.

With each touch and kiss from both men, the pleasure within me built like a raging fire that threatened to consume me completely. And then Ryan kissed a secret spot behind my neck that he knew always drove me wild. That was all it took for the dam of ecstasy to burst and for a powerful orgasm to wash over me.

I held on to Rudy's shoulders for support as my body tensed and shuddered. Both men held me up as I rode out the waves of ecstasy, feeling utterly satisfied but far from fulfilled.

"Wow," I breathed, still trying to catch my breath. "I've never had an orgasm from just kissing before."

Rudy let out a cocky yet endearing chuckle. "You're welcome." I couldn't help but laugh and playfully slap his arm.

Ryan joined in our laughter. "I think I contributed a little bit."

We continued to laugh as I knelt down between the two of them, both of their rock-hard members pointing toward me. My eyes hungrily roamed over them, taking in every detail. Ryan's was always a perfect fit, just the right length for me. But then I saw Rudy's up close, and it was noticeably larger and thicker than Ryan's. My hands seemed to have a mind of their own as they reached up and wrapped around each. My thirst for pleasure guided my mouth first toward Ryan's while my hand stroked Rudy's, feeling the thick veins beneath my fingers that kept him firm and ready.

Every sense in my body was on fire. I'd never been so sexually hungry in my life. Looking up into Rudy's dark eyes, I placed my lips around the head of his throbbing shaft and ran my tongue along the smooth bottom before taking one of his balls into my mouth. I savored the taste of him, slid my tongue back up his length, and took him deeper into my mouth.

The sound of glass clinking together made me open my eyes to see Ryan and Rudy touching their beer bottles in a toast. Laughing, I pulled away from Rudy's cock and continued to stroke both men with fervor.

"Such typical guys," I teased.

But then I couldn't resist anymore. I engulfed Rudy once again. I gagged a few times from his size, but the feeling of power only made me eager to please him.

Ryan's hands caressed my breasts as he knelt down behind me, kissing my neck and shoulders. He whispered in my ear, sending shivers down my spine. "Suck that cock, baby. Suck it hard."

The sound of my husband telling me to pleasure another man excited me beyond belief. My body was so wet with desire that I could almost climax from just the slightest touch. The evidence of my arousal dripped down my thigh, begging for more attention.

Ryan tangled his hand in my hair and guided my mouth back and forth on Rudy's length, controlling the pace. I gagged a few more times before he released me to catch my breath. He then took my elbows in his hands and led me over to the bed, where I lay back with an enthusiastic grin on my face. Rudy's hungry gaze followed us as he lowered himself between my spread thighs.

Meanwhile, Ryan walked around the bed until he stood behind me. His hands roamed over my body as Rudy's lips eagerly found their way to my drenched center. I lost all control and instinctively grabbed onto Rudy's hair, pulling his mouth against me. Already hot and wet, his slick tongue only added fuel to the fire raging inside of me. My hips bucked uncontrollably, and I squeezed my eyes shut as my body tensed and then exploded into a blissful orgasm against Rudy's skilled mouth.

When I opened my eyes, Ryan's throbbing cock hovered at the edge of my mouth, throbbing and glistening with pre-cum. I eagerly took him into my mouth, while Rudy's skilled tongue teased and explored between my legs. I spun into a state of pure bliss.

Suddenly, another orgasm hit me with such force that I couldn't help but cry out, Ryan's cock still in my mouth. This was unheard of for me—three orgasms in one night? But it was all thanks to the way these two men took me to new heights of ecstasy. My body was on fire, every touch sending shockwaves through me.

"Would you like me to wear a condom?" Rudy asked, and though I longed to feel his bare skin against mine, I couldn't risk it with someone so new.

With shaky breaths, I said yes and watched as Ryan handed him a condom from the nightstand. I went back to sucking Ryan fervently, knowing that soon enough Rudy would slide inside of me.

His firm hands raised my legs, exposing my entrance to him. He teased me, rubbing himself through my folds and against my clit. His size took me by surprise, and I had to fight the urge to bite down on Ryan in response. Sensing my reaction, he lightly slapped at my cheek. I quickly let go, mouthing "sorry" as he laughed.

Rudy gradually increased his pace, going deeper and deeper with each thrust, stretching me in ways I never thought possible. The concentrated pressure and fullness only added fuel to the fire within me. Each of Rudy's strokes reignited the passion within me until another intense orgasm washed over me.

Gasping for air, I pushed him out and begged for a moment to catch my breath. Never before had I experienced so many orgasms in one evening, and it was all thanks to these two skilled lovers.

They both lay next to me, caressing my body as I calmed my racing heart.

"How are you enjoying this ride so far?" Rudy asked.

"Everything is fantastic," I said with a grin. "I've never been with two men at once before, and it's overwhelming in the best way possible."

Ryan offered me my beer. I took a few measured sips, the cold liquid soothing my parched throat as I looked down at the two naked men before me. They were both mine to have, all mine. My body was ready for another round.

"Time to switch," I announced with a playful grin.

We all chuckled, and Ryan eagerly moved between my legs. With swift precision, he spread them wide and effortlessly slid into me. Our skin met in familiar union, a perfect fit that sent shivers down my spine. Meanwhile, Rudy had positioned himself in front of me, his hard member pressing against my lips. His boldness and confidence only added to the excitement of the moment.

My body swayed with each powerful thrust from Ryan as Rudy fucked my mouth. The combination of their skilled movements ignited an inferno within me. Ryan pulled my legs back to my shoulders, intensifying the pleasure as he pushed me toward another climax. But I struggled to catch my breath with Rudy's cock filling my mouth.

I pushed away from Rudy, gasping for air, relishing in him filling me. "Switch again," I commanded, feeling a sense of control despite these two men completely dominating me.

Rudy reached for another condom from the nightstand and rolled it onto his impressive length. As I lay on my back, he pushed open my thighs.

"I promise to fuck you hard," he said, his tone dripping with charm and cockiness. His words sent a delicious jolt through my body. I was building toward another orgasm, but there was also something else stirring inside of me, something I'd felt before and tried to suppress.

I cried out as Rudy mercilessly pounded into me, the blend of pain and pleasure pushing me to the brink. I reached for his arms, both wanting him to stop and yet I wanted him to not. But he was relentless, thrusting into me with such force that I couldn't escape. And then I heard him say it—"I'm coming!"—and suddenly I was breaking over the edge I'd been trying to avoid.

I came hard, my body convulsing as fluid squirted out of me onto our soaked sheets. Rudy continued to pound into me, forcing his seed into my depths. Ryan finally released my legs, allowing me to roll into a fetal position as I trembled with aftershocks.

My hand reached out to touch the wet sheets, feeling embarrassed by the mess we'd made. "You've never done that before," Ryan commented in awe.

Despite my embarrassment, I couldn't help but let out a laugh. "Usually when I feel that buildup, it's like I'm about to pee and I want to stop," I admitted, turning my head to give Rudy a narrowed look. "But Rudy didn't stop."

Rudy's smile widened. "I never heard you say stop, otherwise I definitely would have. How did it feel?"

I paused for a moment, thinking back that I never did say stop, and had incredible experience. "It was the most powerful orgasm I've ever had. And I've never had that many in one go."

Rudy and Ryan gave each other a high five, causing me to roll my eyes.

"If I didn't have a condom on, I definitely would have contributed to that wet spot on the sheets," Rudy said with a grin, gesturing toward the large dark patch on the bedspread.

It was an unforgettable experience.

We continued to talk and laugh about more trivial things as we lay naked together in bed, finishing our beers. Eventually, Rudy said he had to leave. He got up from the bed and put his clothes on. Ryan and I put on our robes and walked him to the door. We said goodnight and both expressed our excitement to see him again. He was a fun, easygoing guy with an incredible . . . well-endowed member.

After closing the door behind him, Ryan and I made our way back upstairs, hand in hand. I reached into his robe to stroke his still-hard cock. "You didn't get off yet, did you?" I asked teasingly.

He shook his head, his arousal evident in his eyes.

Without wasting another moment, I kissed him deeply and untied his robe. "Let's take care of that."

We discarded our robes onto the floor and settled onto the bed. I was exhausted from the night's activities but still craved my husband's touch. I feverishly worked his

133

member with my mouth, determined to give him even a fraction of the pleasure I'd just experienced.

While stroking his shaft, I teased and flicked my tongue over his sensitive spot underneath, causing him to moan in pleasure.

Looking up into his eyes, I pulled my mouth off for a moment. "I want it. Come for me, baby," I whispered, knowing exactly what he needed. "I want you. Let me drink your cum."

With that comment, Ryan grabbed my hair and arched back as I closed my lips over him again. His warm seed exploded in my mouth with a ferocity I'd never seen from him before, causing me to gag slightly, but I recovered without taking my mouth off him. The sensation of his cock pulsating was a huge turn-on. The warm sensation filled my mouth so fast I couldn't drink it all.

I pulled back and laughed. "Wow. You were definitely worked up."

"Tonight was one hell of an experience."

Ryan went to the bathroom, cleaned off, and came back to help me change the sheets. "Soaked" was an understatement.

"If we do this again, I'll have to get some mattress protection," I said.

Ryan replied, "If?" His Cheshire grin likely matched mine.

We climbed back into bed and talked for a little while about our new experience.

"You keep asking me what my fantasy would be," I said. "Besides tonight, I think it would be to make out with forty men on my fortieth birthday."

Ryan's eyes lit up with surprise. "Who are you?"

I looked at him and giggled, then leaned over to kiss him softly. "I love you."

"I love you too."

Chapter 13: A Vanilla Oyster Roast

Ryan

Deedee called and asked if we wanted to come over for an oyster roast next weekend. She said it was with a "vanilla" crowd, so there wouldn't be any playing, just good friends.

Vanilla? I could only imagine what other flavors might mean. We said we would be glad to attend their party.

Saturday was cold and rainy for most of the day, but luckily, it stopped before we headed over to Jack and Deedee's. We arrived around four to help set up. Deedee and Jack seemed to be pros at this. The butter was warmed, the tables were set with thick paper covering and oyster knives, a firepit was roaring, and the beer was on ice. Ginger helped Deedee in the kitchen, and I helped Jack with some tables and chairs. There were no discussions of our past encounter; it was just another day with friends.

Gradually, the other guests began to arrive. There were neighbors, relatives, and friends, many of whom we'd met at the crab picking. I was drinking a beer in the garage, waiting for the first batch of oysters to cook on the firepit, when I saw Rudy walk through the door. This was a vanilla party . . . right?

Rudy approached me and shook my hand with his typical laid-back smile. "Hey! What's up?"

"What brings you here?" I asked.

Jack laid down some brown paper on the table. "Rudy brought the oysters."

Ginger and Deedee came out to the garage with some snacks, and Deedee grinned. "Oh, I guess you *know* Rudy already."

Ginger blushed and responded coyly, "Why, yes, I do," and gave him an awkward hug hello.

Swingers blending in with vanillas. Who would have thought? Then I realized: *We* were swingers now! And we blended in with vanilla people all the time, including everyone at Jack and Deedee's last party.

How many swingers are present at other parties, the grocery store, the movie theater . . .? And, more importantly, how can we spot them?

As more people we didn't know came in, Jack and Deedee introduced us as though we were longtime friends. We blended in well, played darts, and traded stories about fishing and hunting. We were having a great time while indulging in some beer and oysters.

Deedee introduced us to their friends, Kurt and Maryann. Kurt was about six feet tall with salt-and-pepper hair in a military cut, and he had a great sense of humor. Maryann had thick shoulder-length hair and was of average height, with generous breasts for her frame—not that I noticed. Much. She was beautiful, and she had an intoxicating smile that transferred to everyone she spoke to.

After she introduced us, Deedee looked around to see if anyone was nearby and whispered, "They're like us."

We all laughed and began vanilla discussions, but because we knew we were all in the lifestyle, there was a little extra flirting. We tried not to make it too obvious.

As we made our way through the crowded bar, Deedee and Jack introduced us to Beth. She was approximately our age, with long, curly blonde hair that cascaded down her slender form. Her figure was accentuated by a low-cut top, revealing her ample bosom. I couldn't help but notice them, although I tried my best not to stare.

Despite her outward attractiveness, it soon became clear that she didn't have much going on upstairs. She spoke in a high-pitched, airy voice and seemed to lack any depth or substance in her conversation. We chatted for a while, but I quickly grew bored and fought the urge to nod off as she prattled on about trivial things.

Eventually, Beth excused herself to grab another drink, and we turned back to Kurt and Maryann. With the help of some Jell-O shots, the conversation flowed easily between us, and we found ourselves laughing and flirting shamelessly. As we finished off our third round of red, green, and purple "jigglers of courage," Jack came over to check on us.

"How's everything going?" he asked with a smile.

"Great!" we all replied enthusiastically.

Jack gestured toward the box of Jell-O shots on the table and laughed. "Just be careful with those triple-X ones. The fruit has been soaked in moonshine."

I raised an eyebrow. This would only add fire to our already intoxicated state.

Not long after that warning, Jack reached behind the table and pulled out a bottle of Wild Turkey. Taking a long swig straight from the bottle, he passed it around for each of us to take a gulp. I hesitated at first, not being much of a whiskey drinker, but I eventually gave in to peer pressure and took a small sip before passing it back to Jack. Maryann eagerly took her turn, tipping the bottle up like a seasoned drinker. But the look on her face afterward immediately told us otherwise.

Before we knew it, she was bolting for the back door, with Ginger quickly following behind her. We could hear retching sounds coming from behind the house, and Kurt shook his head with a chuckle.

"She doesn't handle whiskey or bourbon very well," he explained apologetically.

Jack, Kurt, and I peered around the corner of the house, where Ginger held Maryann's hair as she vomited into the bushes. Ginger looked back at us with a shake of her head, and we knew Maryann was in pretty bad shape.

We went back inside to find Jack holding up the bottle of Wild Turkey with a sly grin. "Anyone else want to take their chances?"

We laughed and I shook my head, knowing my limit had been reached.

"I should probably get my wife home," Kurt announced as he put on his coat and gathered Maryann's things. "I think that changes our plans for the evening."

Ginger came back into the garage, shivering from the cold. "She's really not doing well."

A few minutes later, Kurt returned from dropping off Maryann in the car with a plastic bag in hand. "I guess our night has come to an unexpected end," he said with a sigh.

We walked with him to his car to say goodnight to Maryann, hoping we would have another chance to meet up again. As they drove off, we couldn't help but laugh at how quickly the night had taken a turn for the worse.

After returning to the party, Beth spotted me and made her way over. I tried to avoid her, but she began talking to me, so I felt obligated to listen. To my surprise, she was not a ditzy blonde like I'd initially thought. Her demeanor was completely different from how she appeared earlier. As we talked, I learned she was remarkably intelligent with multiple degrees and a job at a government agency that would impress most people.

"You are incredibly intelligent," I said. "What was with the act earlier?"

"Let's face it, how many people in this crowd enjoy the company of an intelligent woman?" Beth replied.

I chuckled. "Well, my wife and I certainly do, but I understand your point. I wish you'd approached me like this from the start."

"I appreciate a man who enjoys talking to me for my mind rather than just staring at my tits. You wouldn't believe how often men talk to me without even looking at my face."

Feeling emboldened by a few drinks, I responded confidently, "While your tits are certainly worth admiring, I'm much more intrigued by your wit. And I apologize for brushing you off earlier."

As we continued our conversation, I made sure not to bring up anything related to our alternative lifestyle. Despite her stunning appearance, I reminded myself not to let my thoughts wander to images of her naked and bent over a table.

After the majority of guests left, Jack and Deedee suggested that all who remained go inside for a nightcap. So, Ginger and I, Deedee, Jack, Rudy, Beth, and her husband Jim walked into the house.

As soon as we entered the living room, Beth boldly removed her shirt and bra. "Let's get the best part of the night started!"

Ginger and I exchanged surprised looks.

"Well, all right!" Rudy exclaimed.

I looked at Jack and Deedee, confused. *I thought this was a vanilla party?*

"Beth and Jim are not in the lifestyle, but they like to play occasionally," Deedee explained. "You're welcome to stay if you feel comfortable. If not, we understand."

Once again, I followed Ginger's lead as she responded, "Why not?"

Beth removed her pants and kicked off her shoes before kneeling and bending over a lounge chair, her voluptuous breasts filling the seat. She looked at us with a mischievous grin. "Someone better put a cock in me right now!" She positioned her ass in front of me and stared right into my eyes. Ginger leered at me. "Looks like you're being summoned."

The moment was upon us, and my instincts took over. In a flurry of movement, I kicked off my shoes and dropped my pants, reaching for the condom I'd stashed in my pocket before we left the house. Beth spread her smooth thighs, exposing her inviting entrance to me. I dropped to my knees behind her and struggled to push myself into her tight crevice. Frustration turned to laughter as I realized I couldn't penetrate her with ease.

Beth reached back, grasping at her buttocks and trying to open herself wider for me. "I'm extremely tight," she warned. "Just force it slow. It'll fit."

With renewed determination, I pushed myself inside and felt the resistance give way as I entered her depths. She wasn't kidding about being tight. Every inch of my shaft was enveloped in a sensation unlike any other. Gripping her hips, I began to move gently, savoring the feeling of being inside her.

But it was too much. Even with a condom on, I could feel myself getting close to climaxing. Knowing I couldn't hold back any longer, I pulled out.

Beth looked back at me with concern. "What's wrong?"

I was embarrassed to admit that I was close to finishing too soon. I wanted more time with her.

"I want to taste you," I blurted out.

Pulling at her arm, I guided her down onto the floor and gazed at the sight of her beautiful breasts while spreading her legs apart. Lowering my mouth to her sex, I slid my tongue through her folds and sucked on her sweet clit, reveling in the delicious taste of her arousal. As she arched her back and tangled her fingers in my hair, I pushed my tongue deeper inside her but was unable to penetrate fully.

My cock still rock-hard in the condom, I opened her legs wider and slid back into her depth. She gripped me even tighter, and I thrusted with more force, increasing my tempo as she whispered seductively to me.

"Do you like how my tight, wet pussy grips your hard cock? You're making me so wet. Fuck me harder. Pound that little cunt!"

Her words sent shivers of pleasure through me, and I obeyed her command, moving faster and harder until she dug her nails into my ass cheeks and we both cried out in ecstasy as she tightened impossibly around me with her own orgasm. Blushing at how quickly I came, I was relieved that she had also climaxed. It wasn't like me to finish so fast.

As I pulled out, the condom stayed behind, stuck inside her drenched sex. We both laughed as I fished it out.

"Well," she said with a sly smile. "I guess this confirms just how tight I am. It's happened before," she added with a laugh.

Looking up, I saw Ginger enjoying herself with Jack and Rudy in sexual bliss, while Deedee was riding Jim in a

143

nearby chair. Rudy broke away from Ginger and walked over to us. "You're not tired yet, are you?" he asked Beth mischievously.

Her fingers wrapped around his shaft and stroked it with confidence and precision. "Absolutely not." Her voice dripped with desire.

As the two of them began their passionate encounter, I retreated to the kitchen for a cold beer. Then I stood at the counter, took a long swig, and gazed out into the living room. The scene unfolding before me was like something out of a sultry movie. Rudy held Beth against his waist, their bodies locked in an intense rhythm while he thrust into her. I couldn't tear my eyes away from the steamy display. Suddenly, Ginger was beside me, her body pressed against mine as she reached for a sip of my drink.

"Did you enjoy yourself with Beth?" she asked, her voice barely audible over the sounds of pleasure coming from the other room.

I tilted my head, trying to put my thoughts into words. My wife had just asked if I'd enjoyed having sex with another woman. It was surreal. Laughing, I turned to face her. The sight of her naked body pressed against mine in someone else's house with other people present was exhilarating. She smiled but also looked slightly puzzled, no doubt wondering what was going through my mind.

"I did," I replied, pulling her close. "And did you have a good time, baby?"

She whispered back, "At first, Jim couldn't get hard for some reason. But then Deedee joined in, and I moved

144

on to Rudy and Jack, who made sure I was taken care of." She took another drink from my beer and broke into a devilish grin. "I think I'm going to like this."

I raised an eyebrow. "Oh, really?"

We leaned into each other, laughing and kissing as we watched the others still lost in pleasure. Before long, everyone had been satisfied, and we all took turns using the bathroom and getting dressed. As we said our goodbyes, there was a shared sense of joy and sly grins, knowing what had transpired.

Once in the car, Ginger turned to me with wide eyes. "Wow, I didn't expect that," she blurted out.

Over the next few weeks, we continued discussing our newfound lifestyle when alone together. We realized one key factor: the absence of jealousy. We were secure in our love for each other and knew nothing could come between us. With this emotional barrier removed, we were free to explore a whole new world together. A world where we could be open and free with each other, and embrace attention from others who found us desirable.

After many years of marriage, Ginger and I loved each other deeply and had an active sex life. But the feeling of being desired by someone new wasn't as common in a long-term relationship. It's a thrill reminiscent of the early stages of dating. To have someone new crave you, and for you to feel the same way back—it was intoxicating. We talked about this feeling and both agreed that our new adventures were simply an extension of our sex life. It would never replace what we had with each other.

We'd heard so many rumors condemning the swinging practice, denouncing it as immoral, which was why so many people remained discreet. In our society, it seems that "sex" is still an uncomfortable word, so it gets kept in the shadows and whispered about. Our belief is, if more people became more sexually aware and alive (safely), then there would be a lot of happier people in our world today.

Despite this belief, we weren't naive. We got along very well with several neighbors whom we would enjoy evenings with, laughing and chatting over a few beers or glasses of wine, but they knew nothing of our newfound secret life. They were good friends, but we knew that if our secret ever slipped, it would be devastating to those friendships.

So, we decided to live two lives for now.

Chapter 14: Meet & Greet

Ginger

The evening sky was painted with vibrant shades of orange and pink as Ryan and I sat on our back porch. We received a call from our friends Kurt and Maryann, who invited us to join them for a few drinks at the Hitching Post. As we walked into the dimly lit establishment, memories of months past flooded our minds. This was the perfect bar for us—no one from our vanilla life would ever dare to step foot in here.

We spotted Kurt and Maryann sitting at a round table on the other side of the tavern. To our surprise, Jack and Deedee were also with them. We greeted each other warmly before taking a seat. Jack and Deedee explained they'd just happened to be there for dinner at the same time as Kurt and Maryann. Over drinks, we caught up Kurt and Maryann on what they'd missed at the recent oyster roast, while Maryann shared her regret about drinking bourbon, knowing it always made her sick.

As the night went on, Kurt, Maryann, Deedee, and Jack exchanged stories about their own first encounters. The air was filled with laughter as they recounted some awkward moments without ever mentioning names.

One story involved a single woman who'd brought a drunk guy friend to a party, only for him to become even more intoxicated throughout the evening. At one point, he'd ended up naked in a bed, watching his date and several others play around while he played with himself, which was uncomfortable for everyone. Eventually, he got dressed and left without his date, wearing someone else's pants.

Amid the humorous anecdotes, Maryann invited us to attend her birthday party in a couple of weeks at a friend's house.

"Is it a play party?" Deedee asked curiously.

"Absolutely!" Kurt replied with excitement. "What else would we have? Swinging is our life these days. We don't have many vanilla friends left."

Ryan and I exchanged surprised glances. "So," I asked tentatively, remembering the impromptu party at Jack and Deedee's a couple weeks ago. "What exactly happens at this play party?"

Kurt's eyes lit up. "It's like any other birthday party you've been to, but there may be some nudity, some kissing. There will be bedrooms available for those who want to play, and a hot tub outside. Just bring a snack to share, and your own drinks."

Deedee and Jack regretfully declined, unable to make it that evening.

I couldn't help but feel a twinge of unease. "This is a house party?"

"Yes, it's a house party," Kurt confirmed. "That's where the real fun can be had."

I glanced over at Ryan, who seemed to sense my apprehension—for once. "We'll let you know if we can make it."

As we said our goodbyes and went our separate ways with hugs and kisses, I was relieved that Ryan had picked up on my concern.

Driving home in silence, he finally spoke up. "You looked worried about the party. Do we have something else going on that night?"

I paused for a moment, still flashing back to that uncomfortable experience in the creepy basement, unsure whether to laugh or cry at the fact that Ryan had misinterpreted my hesitation as something else.

"Do you not remember the last house party we attended?" I practically screeched. "I don't know if I'm ready for something like that. We had fun with another couple, and then the small, spontaneous party we had at the oyster roast, but the idea of so many people seems a little uncomfortable to me, and the thought of someone's kid being there still haunts me."

Ryan didn't respond, and the silence was deafening. Was I overreacting? Kurt and Maryann were a fun couple, and I believed we would enjoy being with them. But still . . .

Ryan still hadn't said anything.

"Are you upset?" I asked.

Ryan just stared at the road with tightened lips that told me he was thinking of a response. Finally, he said, "Sweetie, let's just talk about it and let them know in a week."

My cell phone chimed with a text message, and when I read it, my face grew warm, like I was a giddy teenager.

"Who was that from?" Ryan asked.

"Kurt. He says it was nice to see us again, and they hope we can go to the party."

"When did he get your number?"

"I gave it to him before we left tonight. That's okay, isn't it?" I knew he'd been bothered by the way I'd been texting Rudy before he knew anything about it, and I didn't want him to get the wrong idea.

"Of course it is, honey. I simply didn't know."

Ryan

As the sun began to rise, Ginger and I sat on the back porch with steaming cups of coffee, discussing our plans for the day. The world around us was waking up. Birds chirped happily, the air was still cool and crisp, and a gentle breeze rustled the leaves on the trees.

Suddenly, Ginger's phone made a familiar "ping" noise, signaling an incoming text message. I couldn't help but ask, "Who's sending you a text so early in the morning?"

With a smitten smile on her face, she replied, "It's Kurt. He texts me every morning to say 'Good morning, sweetie.'"

150

I raised an eyebrow, wondering if their communication was limited to just mornings. As if reading my mind, Ginger grinned and asked playfully, "Jealous?"

A small twinge of insecurity crept into my mind. How much texting had they been doing? And what kind of messages were they exchanging? I took a sip of my coffee to hide my unease.

Ginger noticed my slight discomfort and stood up, placing a comforting hand on my shoulder. "If you think this is personal, then what about us sleeping with other people?" Her voice was calm but disapproving.

She opened the back door and asked if I wanted more coffee. I felt like she'd just slapped me in the face. Was I really feeling jealous? No, that couldn't be it. Just surprised.

When Ginger returned with fresh coffee, she asked hesitantly, "Do you want me to stop texting him?"

I realized that, as we got to know more people, exchanging numbers and sending occasional texts was normal. It should be fine.

"No, sweetie," I reassured her. "But it's something we've never discussed before. I just wasn't expecting it. I think it's fine, but too much of something is never good."

Relief washed over her face, and she beamed gratefully. "Thank you. I appreciate your understanding."

"As long as you don't surprise me with another Rudy situation," I joked, pushing my luck a little. But Ginger's smile remained.

"Fair enough," she said, turning to walk back into the house. "I'm going upstairs to take a shower. Oh, and by the way, Kurt convinced me to go to the party tonight." With a coy smirk, she disappeared inside.

I couldn't help but watch her walk away, noticing the subtle shift of her robe as she moved. She must have sensed my gaze, because she turned around at the bottom of the stairs and asked teasingly, "Are you coming?"

Without hesitation, I jumped up and headed toward her. "Right behind you, sweetie."

"I was hoping you would," she giggled playfully before darting up the stairs with me close behind.

Chapter 15: Our First Real House Party

Ginger

The much-anticipated day of Maryann's party had finally arrived. Two hours before our grand entrance, I found myself frantically tossing clothes all over the bedroom, desperately trying to find the perfect outfit. My half-curled hair was unfinished as I stood next to Ryan, my anxiety escalating.

"We can't go like this," I muttered, shaking my head in defeat. "I don't know what to wear."

Ryan chuckled at my distress. "Did you ask Maryann what she's wearing?"

It was a simple solution that I hadn't even thought of. I immediately called Maryann, and we chatted and laughed as she reassured me that comfort was key for the evening, and that a towel for the hot tub would be a good idea. But then it hit me—she never mentioned bringing swimsuits.

"I didn't think about that!" I exclaimed to Ryan, my panic growing. "What are we going to do?"

Ryan simply laughed and suggested packing one just in case. This whole situation amazed me, especially because the last two times we'd played with other couples had been spontaneous and stress-free.

After much deliberation, I settled on a black skirt and a loose-fitting blouse that showed off more cleavage than I'd normally dare to reveal in public. With my hair now fully curled, I turned to see Ryan dressed in his usual button-down shirt, khaki pants, and dress shoes.

"You guys have it so easy," I grumbled jokingly as we prepared to leave. We loaded everything into the car and climbed in, only for Ryan to ask me if everything was okay.

Before I could respond, I received a text that made me burst out laughing. "Yup, everything's okay," I said with a smile.

With curiosity, Ryan glanced down at my phone and then back up at me with a mischievous glint in his eye. "Is that Kurt telling you he has a hard-on with your name on it?"

We both laughed as we drove off, eagerly anticipating what the night had in store for us.

On the way to the party, we discussed our boundaries and rules: How would we interact with other couples without upsetting each other? As newcomers to the swinging scene, this was our first real house party, and we had no idea what to expect. Ryan deferred to me on setting the rules, since I was more hesitant about diving into the unknown.

"Let's stick together at first," I suggested, "and meet other couples. If we find a couple we're both interested in, then we can go off together to play, but only if we both agree. We won't just take one for the team if only one of us is attracted to someone else."

Ryan couldn't help but laugh at my rule-making.

"Don't laugh, I'm serious! I don't want you to find some attractive girl, and then I find out I'm not attracted to her husband. Don't put me in that position . . . please?" My heart pounded at the thought.

Ryan agreed with a reassuring glint in his eye, which eased my anxiety. "What about us going off to play with someone solo?"

I shot him a pointed glare. "Don't you dare leave me alone. It's our first party, so let's just take it easy, and learn, and stick together."

He nodded.

I reached into my purse and pulled out a packet of condoms. "Here, in case you forgot them."

Ryan chuckled.

"We use protection . . . okay?"

He agreed, still smiling. "How long have you kept condoms in your purse?"

"I just put them in there from the nightstand. I don't want to take any chances."

"What about while we're downstairs? Are we locked at the hip, or do we drift around and strike up conversations with others?"

"Let's stay together for a while until I'm comfortable," I answered.

As we arrived at the house, we saw what looked like forty cars parked along the road. The sheer number of cars stunned me, and I gripped Ryan's hand.

"Relax," he said soothingly. "I'm sure some of the cars belong to the neighbors."

I frowned but stepped out of the car. The house was a lovely two-story home nestled in a beautiful middle-class neighborhood with paved streets, lush pear and cherry trees dotting the yards, and meticulously maintained landscaping. Music wafted from the backyard, adding to the already lively atmosphere.

We rang the doorbell and were greeted by a lovely red-haired woman with a warm smile.

"Hi, I'm Trish. Welcome to our home! I don't think we know you. What are your names?"

"We're Ryan and Ginger," Ryan responded. "Kurt and Maryann invited us."

Ryan

Maryann burst into the foyer with glee, arms outstretched. "Ginger! You made it!" We both offered birthday wishes and thanked Trish, our hostess, for letting us inside.

Maryann took Ginger's hand and led her farther into the house. "Come on in and have a birthday drink with me." I watched as they disappeared into the crowd, wondering if Ginger would be comfortable without my presence.

Trish turned to me, her eyes sparkling mischievously. "Well, it seems like your wife is in good hands. Is this your first time at a house party?"

I nodded a bit nervously.

Trish squeezed my hand playfully and gave me a flirtatious smile. "Don't worry, I'll introduce you to some of our friends."

As we walked around the party, I noticed the theme was a Hawaiian luau, which we hadn't been aware of beforehand. We strolled into the open-concept living room, where I could see Ginger in the kitchen, enjoying a shot with Maryann. I couldn't help but wonder if she would get drunk too quickly.

Trish introduced me to several of her friends, but I leaned in close and whispered, "I apologize in advance if I forget anyone's name."

She winked at me slyly. "No worries, you'll probably see them again. And if you ever get that close to my ear again, you'd better kiss me first."

I was taken aback by her boldness, and my cheeks flushed. She grinned at me knowingly before turning to point out the stairs leading to the bedrooms. Giving me some quick rules, she emphasized the importance of respect and consent in this environment.

"Just remember, no means no, and don't be pushy or aggressive. And definitely don't be a Creepy Guy."

My mind immediately conjured up images of a sleazy man in a trench coat, and I shuddered at the thought of being compared to him. I raised an eyebrow with a slight chuckle. "What exactly constitutes a 'Creepy Guy?' I just want to make sure I stay far away from that title."

Trish laughed and gave me a playful pat on the arm. "Something tells me you won't need to worry about that."

She flashed a coy grin and began to unbutton my shirt. Her fingers moved deftly down the fabric, revealing glimpses of bare skin as she went. "A Creepy Guy is someone who just creeps around, staring at people . . ."

Continuing with the next two buttons, she ran her hand along my chest until it rested on my bare skin. Her touch sent a shiver through me. "Not really talking to anyone, grabbing girls without permission, that sort of guy," she explained, still caressing my chest.

Her eyes met mine, and she added with a hint of flirtation, "You know, you're kind of cute." And then she leaned in to kiss me.

I couldn't resist reaching up to tangle my fingers in her hair as our lips pressed together. The taste of her was intoxicating, and I eagerly deepened the kiss, savoring the feeling of her tongue dancing against mine. Our bodies pressed closer together, and I lost myself in how much I wanted this woman right now. However, a small part of me was apprehensive about what I could, or should, do. I didn't want to come across as a Creepy Guy.

But then Trish took my hand and placed it under her loose blouse. With no bra underneath, I felt the softness of her breast directly against my palm. My arousal grew even more evident, and I gently caressed her breast, relishing in the feel of her responding to my touch. My hand drifted farther south through the bright-green grass skirt to the center of her thighs, but she pulled away slightly.

"No, no, no," she said playfully, panting slightly from our passionate kissing session. "Be patient. The lady will let you know when you can go there." She bit her lower lip seductively and shook her head slowly while glancing at my barely contained arousal. "I have to play hostess, but I hope to get to know you a lot better soon."

I watched her walk away with both frustration and excitement. I could definitely get used to these parties. Making my way to the kitchen, I noticed Ginger doing another shot. She was going to be pretty wasted soon.

I walked up to her and Maryann, who was also downing shots. "How's the birthday girl?" I asked.

Maryann turned to me with an empty shot glass, a big smile on her face. "Great!" Then she introduced me to her other friends, signaling this would be quite the party.

Mark and Debbie stood out among the crowd, their physical differences stark. The tall, broad-shouldered man was over six feet tall, his blond hair catching the sunlight. Debbie, on the other hand, was petite, probably no taller than five feet. Her figure was perfectly shaped, with round breasts almost too perfect to be natural. Her wavy blonde hair cascaded down her shoulders in a careless yet alluring manner. She wore a bikini top and a floral skirt that matched Maryann's outfit.

I placed my hand gently on Ginger's back and guided her through the lively crowd. "Let's take a walk around and see the rest of the house," I said.

Maryann leaned over to give Ginger a goodbye kiss. "Go have fun. We'll catch up later."

As we strolled away, I whispered to Ginger, "You might want to pace yourself with the drinks."

"I know, but they keep offering them to me, and I don't want to be rude," she replied sheepishly.

We made our way through the living area and up the stairs. Ginger looked at me curiously. "Where are we going?"

"I just want to peek upstairs and see if anything interesting is happening. We can come right back down," I reassured her.

We stopped in front of a closed door, where the muffled moans of passionate lovemaking resounded from behind it. The next door was slightly open, inviting us inside. We cautiously peeked in to find two couples entwined on the bed, lost in each other's embrace.

"Remember our first time with Jack and Deedee?" I whispered to Ginger.

She playfully nudged me with her elbow. "Shh."

We watched for a moment, enthralled by the erotic scene before us. Suddenly, one of the women noticed us and signaled for us to join them.

Ginger smiled politely and whispered back, "Maybe another time."

She took my hand and led me back downstairs.

"Why didn't you want to join them? They invited us," I asked curiously. I think I knew the answer but wanted to be sure. People don't meet that scenario often, and as open-minded as we'd become, I found it intriguing.

Her grip on my hand tightened, and she came to a halt, locking her penetrating gaze on mine. "I just don't want to sleep with random people. I want to at least get to know them a little bit first."

I understood her perspective, but I couldn't deny the arousal coursing through my body like a teenager with a crush.

We made our way outside to the backyard, where a lively group of about twenty people were gathered around tables and a hot tub. A large tree stood tall in the middle of the deck, its branches reaching up toward the sky. Four couples lounged in the hot tub, and others mingled around the table, all laughing and kissing. Everyone was clearly having a great time.

I leaned down to whisper in Ginger's ear. "Definitely a different experience from that basement party."

She let out a laugh and playfully elbowed me. "Please never remind me of that again."

Placing my hand on Ginger's back, I gently nudged her toward the invitingly warm hot tub.

She paused, uncertain, and turned to me. "I'm not sure I'm ready for that," she whispered. I nodded, and we walked back into the bustling house.

As we entered the main living area, Kurt spotted us and made his way over with a friendly smile. "Hi! Are you having a good time so far?"

"Absolutely!" we replied in unison, exchanging excited glances.

Kurt and Ginger engaged in conversation for a few moments while my mind wandered. I told Ginger I was going to get a drink and explore the rest of the house. She nodded, clearly comfortable with talking to Kurt alone.

161

Making my way to the kitchen, I grabbed a cold beer from our cooler and scanned the room. The lively atmosphere was infectious, with people socializing in every corner. But my eyes were drawn to a small den just off the kitchen, where two stunning women lay naked on the floor, wrapped up in each other's embrace. My youthful eagerness consumed me as I watched them kiss and touch each other. They noticed me standing there with a beer in hand, and they smiled before returning to their passionate exchange.

But then it hit me—I didn't want to be seen as a Creepy Guy gawking at them. So I tore my gaze away and left the den, imprinting the image of those beautiful women on my memory.

Back in the kitchen, Maryann was still handing out shots like candy. "Here, Ryan," she said enthusiastically, thrusting a shot glass toward me. "Do a birthday shot with me."

I obliged and clinked glasses with her before throwing back the butterscotch schnapps. But before I could even process the taste, Maryann surprised me with a passionate kiss. Instinctively, I relaxed myself into it. She was a fantastic kisser.

But just as quickly as it started, she pulled away with a giddy smirk. "Wow, your wife taught you how to kiss really well," she said. "I'm glad you two made it tonight."

I couldn't help but be confused. Did my wife teach me how to kiss? Since when? But I didn't question her. "Thanks for inviting us," I said.

162

Heading back into the living room, my eyes scanned the crowd for Ginger. But she wasn't where I'd left her. As I walked farther into the room, I recognized her outfit on the sofa but couldn't see her face, as it was buried between Kurt's legs. My heart skipped a beat as I registered what was happening—this was breaking our rules. Her own rule.

Deciding to step outside for some fresh air, and perhaps find a distraction, I tried not to dwell on what was happening between Ginger and Kurt. If she was already comfortable enough to break our rules, maybe adapting to this lifestyle would be easier than we'd expected. My gaze was immediately drawn to the steamy hot tub, and I walked up to it. The sight of Maryann's naked body as it gracefully entered the water alongside her friends, Jackie and Terra, was enough to make my heart skip a beat. We had briefly met earlier in the kitchen, but seeing them in all their unclothed glory was an entirely different experience.

Maryann's figure was nothing short of breathtaking as she stepped down into the water, her movements fluid and sensual. Her flawless skin glistened under the warm glow of the spa lights, and I couldn't tear my eyes away as she submerged herself into the water.

But Maryann and her friends were not the only ones enjoying a nude dip in the hot tub. Another guy, Justin, sat on the other end of the tub, his muscular frame also bare for all to see. Surprisingly, I found myself remembering his name from our earlier introduction—perhaps due to the thrill of seeing everyone sans clothing.

"Come join us, Ryan," Maryann beckoned with a mischievous glint in her eye. "We won't bite . . . hard." Her words were followed by a chorus of giggles from Jackie and Terra.

Despite Ginger breaking rules with Kurt, surely getting naked with these beautiful ladies in a hot tub wouldn't be too much of a transgression.

Before I even realized it, my shirt was off and my shoes were discarded. Jackie playfully warned me not to "break anything important" while removing my clothes, and I laughed along with everyone else as I made my way up the ladder and into the steaming water.

"Just stay like that for a while," Jackie teased as I settled into a corner next to Justin, Terra joining in with comments admiring my exposed state. Jackie then turned to Maryann. "Who is he?"

"He and his wife, Ginger, are new friends of ours. They're brand-new to the lifestyle," Maryann explained, raising her drink in a toast. Jackie and Terra followed suit, welcoming me into their group.

I raised my beer in return, grateful for their acceptance but unsure of what I was supposed to do now. Justin seemed just as unsure, but we were soon transfixed by the sight of Jackie and Maryann making out while Terra showered them with kisses on their shoulders. It was like watching a sensual dance, and we sat there, entranced as we sipped our beers and watched these beautiful women kiss and caress each other.

Some time later, Ginger made her way over to us. "So, this is where you're hiding."

Maryann motioned for Ginger to join us in the hot tub. "Time to get naked, missy!"

Ginger blushed but hesitantly obliged as Terra and Jackie encouraged her. I couldn't deny that I was eager to see my wife join in on the fun.

"I'll need another shot before I can do that," she admitted.

As if on cue, Trish appeared with a tray of colorful Jell-O shots in hand. "Here's your shot. Now get naked!"

We all laughed as Ginger expertly downed her shot and took a deep breath before stripping off her clothes and joining us in the hot tub. My eyes never left hers as she made her way down the ladder and into the water, her naked body finally joining ours as we basked in the warm, bubbling water of the spa.

Terra, Jackie, and Maryann immediately pulled Ginger closer to their side of the tub, their hands and lips all over her body, caressing her skin, and teasing her breasts. My jaw dropped in shock, and I nearly dropped my beer as well. Even Justin seemed taken aback.

Ginger had always said she was strictly into men, but watching her switch between each of these beautiful women, kissing and touching them with passion and skill, made me question everything I knew about her. I took in every little detail—the way Ginger's body moved under their touch, the sounds of pleasure escaping their lips, the taste of my beer on my tongue.

"Come here and hold Ginger up for me," Terra called out to me suddenly.

165

Without hesitation, I floated toward them and placed my hands under Ginger's hips, lifting her thighs out of the water. Terra wasted no time going down on Ginger, expertly using her tongue to bring my wife pleasure. As I held Ginger steady, Terra looked up at me with a sly grin as she dined on my wife. It was a front-row seat to a show I never wanted to end.

But eventually, my arms burned from holding Ginger up in this position. Terra struggled to stay on task as Ginger's thighs dipped below the water a few times, and I finally had to lower Ginger back down into the water.

Terra looked to me with a mischievous glint in her eye. "Stand up."

Without hesitation, I stood at attention upon her command, not realizing another part of me was at attention also. As though scripted in a porn film, she grabbed my cock and aggressively sucked on it. The sensation was unexpected. She maintained eye contact with me, a smirk playing on her lips as she expertly used her tongue and lips to pleasure me.

After what seemed like an eternity, but also not long enough, Terra glided back to the ladies, grabbed her drink, and casually said, "Welcome to the lifestyle, guys!"

I sat back down in the water, still in shock from what had just happened, and gratefully grabbed my beer. As I took a long sip, I realized how parched I was.

"Thanks for the very, *very* warm welcome!" Ginger exclaimed with a smile.

We continued talking and getting to know each other better while enjoying the warm water and company of our new friends. Eventually, Ginger announced she was getting too warm and needed to get out of the spa. Justin, Maryann, and Terra followed suit, leaving me alone in the water with my thoughts and my beer.

As I stood up and walked toward the step, Jackie waded in front of me. Her body glistened in the moonlight, wet from the warm water of the spa.

"Where are you going?" she asked, her lips slightly parted with eagerness in her eyes.

Who was I to pass that up? I settled down to where she was, and we began kissing. Our tongues danced as we explored each other's mouths with a passionate fervor. I flinched at the sharp pain in my lower lip as she bit down on it, hard enough to make it bleed. But the pain quickly faded as we continued our heated kisses.

I reached up to caress her breasts, gently fondling and squeezing them as our lips remained locked together. After a minute, I dared to slide my hand lower, over her mound and through her crevice. She opened her legs wider, giving me permission to slip my fingers inside of her. My cock throbbed with arousal, so hard I swore the skin would split open.

Sliding my two long fingers into her, I finger-fucked her slowly at first, then built up speed and intensity. Her hips gyrated deliberately, and she let out a low moan that grew louder with each thrust of my fingers. To add to her pleasure, I rubbed the base of my palm against her clit with every thrust.

Jackie responded by kissing me harder and more aggressively. Finally, she closed her eyes and arched her back, turning her face to the stars as she climaxed. I held onto her to keep her from falling backward as her body shuddered with pleasure.

Once she regained her composure, she kissed me again with a smile. "That was good," she said huskily. "Now sit up on the side of the spa."

Without hesitation, she took my throbbing erection into her mouth. I grabbed and fondled her breasts as she aggressively worked on my shaft, swirling her tongue around the head before sucking harder. She devoured my cock with such determination and skill that I felt myself nearing the edge. I warned her that I wouldn't be able to last much longer if she kept going like this, but she only sucked harder and faster.

Suddenly, Jackie looked up at me while stroking my shaft. "I want it. Come for me," she said eagerly.

With a low growl, I felt my body quake. "Fuck! Here I come!" My dick pulsated as I shot warm semen into her mouth. She continued to suck, swallowing every drop with enthusiasm. As my orgasm subsided, her motions slowed, and she pulled her mouth off me, kissing my still-sensitive shaft leisurely from the bottom all the way to the tip. Jackie beamed proudly and leaned in to kiss me again.

Reaching over to grab her drink, she said, "Thank you, that was pretty hot."

I didn't know what to say. She had just given me an incredible blow job, and now she was thanking *me?*

"You should have felt it from my end," I managed to say between heavy breaths.

She laughed. "Oh, I felt every drop go down my throat."

Blushing at her boldness, I welcomed her kiss.

"Let's go cool down," Jackie suggested as she stood up in front of me. Water droplets cascaded down her body, accentuating her erect nipples and leading my gaze downward to her bald glory mere inches away from my face. This was the first time I had seen her entire body, and she was gorgeous—shapely figure, green eyes, and auburn hair. In that moment, I wanted nothing more than to keep exploring every inch of her.

As we got out of the spa, I realized we didn't have any towels. Jackie had her towel on a nearby chair, and luckily, Trish happened to walk by and notice my predicament. "Hold on a minute, I'll get you a towel," she offered kindly.

As I stood there, the cool night air caressed my bare skin while I held a cold beer in my hand. My eyes scanned the group of people around me, all completely at ease and comfortable with their nudity. It was like something out of a dream, everyone accepting and respectful of one another's bodies.

Trish returned with a fluffy towel and offered it to me with a gentle smile, her eyes flickering down to take in my nude form before meeting mine again. "Oh yes, we definitely need to see more of you," she purred and placed a soft kiss on my lips before handing me the towel.

Drying off quickly, I slipped back into my clothes and made my way into the house, where Ginger and Kurt were chatting in the living room. Still elated from my hot tub experience, I floated toward them, only to see Kurt walk away as I approached.

"Is everything okay?" Ginger asked me. "Kurt thought you might have been upset when you were watching us earlier."

I grinned and wrapped my arm around her waist. "Oh, that? That's already forgotten. It may have bothered me at first, since you broke your own rules within minutes after we arrived. But after what just happened, it's no big deal."

"I'm sorry," Ginger said. "We were discussing our sexual preferences, and blow jobs came up. I couldn't resist showing off my deep-throating skills." Then she leaned in and whispered in my ear, "I hope my little show in the hot tub made up for it."

I couldn't help but smile. It definitely had. As we sipped our drinks and headed toward the kitchen, Trish pointed out an older gentleman with gray hair, who seemed to wander aimlessly around the party. She mentioned that no one knew who he was.

We watched as he approached a slightly drunk woman and kissed her before reaching his hand between her legs. She quickly pushed him away with a smile and walked off.

Trish's eyes narrowed in suspicion. "We can't have a Creepy Guy at our party." She marched over to confront him and make sure he left the party immediately.

I stepped over to where a well-dressed woman sat in the kitchen. Her long gray-and-black dress exuded a conservative air, almost out of place in the swinging atmosphere of the party. "Hello," I introduced myself, extending my hand. "I'm Ryan. Are you here alone?"

She shook my hand politely. "No, my husband is around here somewhere. I'm just waiting for him to finish whatever he's up to."

A sudden unease crept over me as I turned to look to where she was focused, only to find a man passionately kissing Maryann. His hand had slipped under her miniskirt, prompting her to push him away and scold him for being too forward.

The room fell silent as all eyes turned to the awkward couple. The man, who appeared to fall into the "Creepy Guy" definition by some guests, then grabbed his wife's hand and announced loudly, "I'm going to fuck my wife now. Who wants to join us?"

Needless to say, there were no takers. Ginger and I quickly made our way outside to avoid the uncomfortable scene.

A few minutes later, Trish joined us outside. "I asked the couple to leave and suggested they do some research on proper etiquette at swinger parties."

171

Feeling guilty about my own initial clumsiness when attempting to kiss Trish, I blushed and resolved to be more respectful in the future.

As we walked around the outdoor area, we struck up conversations with other couples and heard stories of their experiences in the swinging lifestyle. No one mentioned any names, but it was enlightening to learn from their encounters and keep an eye out for similar situations.

Before we knew it, it was already 2:00 a.m. and the festivities were winding down. Ginger and I were exhausted and had a long drive home. Trish kindly offered us a room to spend the night in, but we politely declined.

As we made our way to our cars, Kurt and Maryann accompanied us. After hugging and thanking Ginger for coming to her birthday party, Maryann pulled her into a long kiss that escalated into full-on making out.

Kurt and I exchanged knowing glances, enjoying the sight but also eager to get some rest. Before parting ways, I thanked Kurt for inviting us, and for his guidance throughout the week leading up to the party.

Kurt laughed. "Yeah, these parties can be intimidating if you're new and don't know anyone. But I thought you two could handle it. Did you have a good time?"

"Absolutely!" I replied with enthusiasm.

Amid the sounds of passionate moaning from Ginger and Maryann's direction, "Me too!" Ginger added.

We said our goodbyes and got into the car. As we drove away from the party, Ginger and I looked at each other and exclaimed in unison, "Wow!"

#

The next evening, we went to visit our neighbors, Mercedes and Chet, for some wine and hors d'oeuvres. They were some of our closest neighbor-friends, and we enjoyed getting together with them. We had so many similarities. Well, perhaps not as many, given our new interests. We talked over wine and bourbon about the normal things going on in our lives, from work, what was happening in town, what the other neighbors were doing, our kids' lives, and global problems.

Chet poured some more wine while Mercedes squinted, looking at us up close. "Wow, you guys are looking ragged. Have you been staying up late?"

Ginger and I looked at each other. "We were up late at a birthday party last night," I said.

"Oh, fun. Whose birthday was it?" Mercedes asked.

We looked each other again. I realized we were building our own trap. "Our friends, Kurt and Maryann. We haven't had them over to our house yet," I said, wanting to change the topic quickly. "How's your new job coming along?"

Mercedes's eyes lit up. She loved to boast about her achievements.

We chatted for a while longer about all sorts of things, from car maintenance to the algae growth in the lake, to techniques for smoking meat on the grill.

173

Eventually, we had to leave because it was late and we had to work the next day. We exchanged hugs as we always did—not the same types of hugs we'd grown accustomed to—and headed home.

"Wow, that was close," Ginger said on the way. "What if we have too much to drink and let something slip?"

We exchanged wide-eyed looks. Mercedes would freak out.

I said, "Well, then they can join us if they want."

We both laughed, knowing full well that would never happen. Chet and Mercedes were some of the best friends and neighbors anyone could ever ask for, but this lifestyle was definitely not something to spring on them, especially with how conservative they were.

Chapter 16: Called Out

Ginger

The next day, I was back at work in my cramped office, surrounded by piles of paperwork, and constantly interrupted by ringing phones and buzzing emails. The chaos of the day made it feel like I'd been away from work for months.

My colleague, Deadra, was busy rifling through the file cabinets outside my office, the metallic screeching reverberating off the walls. I had asked multiple times for someone to oil them, but it seemed like Deadra had a lot of filing to do and didn't have time for such trivial tasks.

Suddenly, the noise stopped and an eerie silence filled the room. When I turned to look at the door, Deadra's curious gaze met mine.

I tilted my head and flashed her a smile. "What's on your mind?"

"There's something different about you," she said, puzzled.

I quickly checked my blouse for any coffee spills, worried that my hectic morning may have left me looking disheveled. "What do you mean?"

"I don't know . . . you just seem to have this happy glow about you," she exclaimed. "Wait a minute. Are you pregnant?"

I burst out laughing. "No way, I'm definitely not pregnant. I'm just in a good place right now."

She smiled knowingly. "Okay, but I'll be keeping an eye on you," she joked before returning to her duties.

As I sat there, pondering her observation, I realized she may be onto something. Lately, I'd been feeling happier and more content in general, despite the overwhelming workload on my desk. It was no surprise after such an amazing weekend with Ryan.

I couldn't resist calling him to share what Deadra had said.

"Don't worry about it," he reassured me. "I've noticed you're in a better mood too. Maybe it's because of your husband giving you some fabulous loving."

I couldn't help but roll my eyes. "You're incorrigible. Did you see my eye roll through the phone?"

We both laughed before hanging up. As I finished up my work and grabbed my lunch from the microwave, I noticed Deadra walking by my office more frequently than usual. Every time she passed, she shot me a knowing smile before continuing on her way. Something was definitely going on.

As I sat down to eat my leftover lasagna at my desk, Deadra entered my office and took a seat in the chair across from me. "I know what it is," she said with a mischievous glint in her eye.

She paused for a dramatic effect and stared at me intently.

I slowly twirled a forkful of steaming pasta toward my open mouth. I couldn't wait to take a bite, but then her words hit me like a punch in the gut.

176

"You're a swinger, aren't you?" the words hung in the air, heavy with judgment and shock.

My eyes widened in surprise and my muscles tensed. Gently setting the fork down, I forced myself to swallow the unchewed food before responding. My mind raced, wondering how this woman had come to such a conclusion. Did she have inside information? Did I unknowingly give off some kind of vibe?

Slowly standing up from my seat, I walked around my desk until I stood next to Deadra. "Come with me," I murmured, trying to keep my voice calm.

As we stepped outside into the warm sunshine, I guided us around the corner of our office building, away from any prying eyes or ears.

"Is that really something you want to discuss in the workplace?" I spoke through clenched teeth, my face flushing with embarrassment and anger.

But instead of apologizing, Deadra seemed excited by her assumption. "You are, aren't you?" she exclaimed.

Struggling to maintain composure, I replied firmly. "Even if I were, it's not appropriate to talk about at work. If you want to discuss this further, let's go out for lunch tomorrow. But please do not mention this to anyone else, or make any comments like that again."

Deadra quickly apologized and promised not to bring it up again. We agreed to meet for lunch the next day and discuss things more calmly.

The rest of the day was a blur as I avoided phone calls and emails, too stressed and anxious to focus on work.

177

By the time Ryan came home later that evening, I was practically pacing a hole into the kitchen floor. Pouring myself a glass of pinot grigio, my usual stress-reliever, I tried to calm down and gather my thoughts.

As soon as Ryan walked through the door, I rushed over to him. "Deadra asked me if I'm a swinger today, and I'm freaking out!" I blurted out.

"What? Slow down. What happened?" he asked, concern etched on his face.

I explained the situation to him and my plan to meet Deadra for lunch tomorrow.

"Wow, looks like someone had a good time this weekend," Ryan teased with a mischievous grin.

Despite my worries, his joke made me laugh, and I couldn't help but playfully slap his arm. "It's not funny!" I protested, trying to stifle my own laughter.

Ryan's expression turned serious. "Maybe she's in the lifestyle too," he suggested. "Or maybe she's just curious and took a chance in asking. Our profile picture does kind of look like you . . . with your head cut off, of course." He chuckled lightly. "Just see what she knows first before disclosing anything. And make sure she understands this is not a topic for discussion at work."

I hesitantly agreed, my nerves churning my stomach. I knew I would need some melatonin to help me sleep that night.

As I got ready for bed, a sense of unease crept over me. How did this happen? We had taken precautions and been discreet. The thought of losing my job over this made my heart race.

While washing my face, I caught a glimpse of myself in the mirror, and it hit me. Why was I so nervous? This wasn't the same as cheating on my husband. I was a valuable employee, praised by management at work. There was no reason for me to be scared or apprehensive about this situation. Instead, I should be taking control and leading the way.

The melatonin took longer than expected, but eventually, I fell into a restless sleep.

The next morning, I still felt uneasy. Sipping my coffee on the back porch, I watched the sun rise over the rippling water, trying to calm my racing thoughts. What would I say to Deadra? And why couldn't I shake the embarrassment?

As I got dressed for work, I reminded myself there was nothing shameful about what Ryan and I were doing. We were simply expanding our intimate life with others. It was no one else's business but ours. And besides, it was Deadra who had brought it up in the first place. I wasn't going around telling everyone about it unprompted.

Arriving at the office, I set down my bag and headed to our small coffee bar, where Deadra was already waiting with a steaming cup in hand.

"Hi Ginger, looking forward to lunch today," she greeted me with her usual friendly smile.

I paused for a moment, unsure of what to say, but also unable to deny how attractive she looked in her tight-fitting maroon dress that hugged her petite figure. The thought crossed my mind that Ryan would certainly be interested in her. I scolded myself for even thinking of her in that way.

But then I grinned and replied, "Me too. Let's plan for eleven o'clock."

Deadra agreed, and I tried to focus on my work, catching up on tasks that I'd neglected the day before. But as the morning went on and I dealt with a few difficult customers, I realized it was already lunchtime.

Deadra peeked into my office. "Ready? I'll drive."

Taking a deep breath, I grabbed my purse and joined her. As we walked out together, my nerves still flared up, but I forced a smile. "Let's go."

The café was a small soup-and-sandwich shop that was always quite loud during the lunch rush. We ordered our meals and headed to a small table in the corner.

As soon as we sat down, Deadra excitedly said, "So, tell me all about it."

I laughed. "What do you know so far? And what makes you think I am one?"

"I've seen you happy a few times when you were in the office, and usually only people who are sexually active are that happy." She took a sip of her drink, then took a big breath like she was preparing herself. "I've been curious about the swinging lifestyle for a little while, so I've looked on a website and scanned the local area to learn more. And then . . . I came across you and your husband's profile. Except I didn't realize it was you at first, since you cropped

180

your heads out of the picture. But then I remembered seeing that same picture when you showed a few pics from a Halloween party a while back, so I took a chance in asking. You really wouldn't make a good poker player."

I sat there with my mouth hanging open, stunned. "Wow, you should have been a detective."

We both laughed.

Our lunch arrived, and Deadra said, "So, tell me all about it. When did you start? How long have you been involved? Do you get into girls too?"

"Whoa—slow down." She was so eager and full of questions. "So, you're not in this lifestyle?"

"No, but I like sex a lot, and I really want to try a few things that I've heard happen with swingers. I've read a lot but have never been brave enough to try."

Okay, so she was just curious. I took a bite of my sandwich, then a sip of my drink, and collected my thoughts. "Okay, now that the cat is out of the bag, what would you like to know?"

We had a long chat and developed a good understanding. I briefly told her my experience so far, and she was intrigued. I found out she was on SLS as well. I gave her our screen name and said to ask us questions if she had any but to keep the discussion outside the office. She promised, and we went back to work.

Back at work, I got very little done as I stared through my computer monitor. *How many other people out there are in the lifestyle, or are curious about it, and we would never know?*

Deadra's enthusiasm was far greater than mine had been when we first started, but she was single and full of energy.

When I got home, I told Ryan what happened.

"No way!" He laughed. "How funny is that? When are you inviting her over?"

I slapped his arm—but we both laughed.

After dinner, we sat on the back porch, sipping some Merlot.

"I wonder how many other people are out there in the lifestyle, and we would never know?" Ryan said.

I laughed. "I've thought the same thing."

For such a potentially dramatic experience, I was glad and relieved it had ended on a positive note.

Chapter 17: On the List

Ginger

The months drifted by, filled with sporadic texts and emails from the friends who shared our lifestyle. We even went on a couple of friend dates, like wine tasting with Deedee and Jack, accompanied by another flirty couple they knew. But for the most part, our lives returned to their vanilla state. No playdates or parties—just the mundane routine of work and home.

One day, Maryann's message lit up my phone screen, announcing a house party hosted by their friends Debbie and Mark. I vaguely recalled meeting them at Maryann's birthday bash, but she assured me they were good friends with Jackie. A tinge of heat crept into my cheeks as I remembered Jackie's company in the hot tub. I called Maryann back.

She answered on the first ring, her voice buzzing with excitement. "So, can you make it?"

"I'm not sure. I'll have to talk to Ryan," I replied.

"Well, it looks like you guys are on the list," she exclaimed.

"The list?"

"Yeah, the list of people who everyone wants at their parties. Word spreads quickly in this lifestyle—almost like high school rumors."

I wasn't sure how to feel about being talked about in such a way. "I guess that's a good thing?"

Maryann laughed merrily. "It's great! You'll be invited to all the best parties now. The first one is usually a test to see if you're friendly, fun, and drama-free. Let me know if you can come. It's this Saturday, and you usually have to be approved before attending, so make your decision tonight."

After hanging up, I couldn't help but wonder what kind of rumors had spread about us in this tight-knit community. Were we being judged? Praised? This thought lingered as I prepared Ryan's favorite dinner: pork tenderloin, with a side of roasted potato slices covered with cheese and herbs. As the aroma filled the house, I couldn't shake off the feeling of being under a microscope.

When Ryan arrived home from work, I welcomed him with a kiss before ushering him to the table set with candles as soft music played in the background.

He raised an eyebrow in surprise at the fancy dinner setting. "So, what's going on? What do you want?" he quipped.

I blushed, my cheeks burning hot. "I just wanted to do something nice for you, honey."

He gave me a knowing look but didn't press further, and instead, we enjoyed our dinner together.

Afterward, we settled on the back porch with a glass of wine to watch the sun dip below the horizon. As we sipped our drinks, I told Ryan about the party invitation. The thought of us being the topic of discussion in this lifestyle made me uneasy, but I brushed it off and focused on enjoying this moment with my husband.

He sat up, his deep gaze meeting mine. "So, you said yes, right?"

I should have anticipated this question.

"I said that I would talk to you about it, but she mentioned something strange. Apparently, all the regular couples at these parties were discussing us, and it seems we've made it onto the coveted party list."

"Yes!" Ryan exclaimed with excitement, pumping his arm as if he'd just won a major golf tournament.

I gave him a stern look. "Did you hear what I said? People were talking about us. Should we expect this every time we attend one of these events?"

"Well," Ryan said with a shrug. "In this lifestyle, it's not surprising that they're talking about new people. But we're easygoing and drama-free, and we don't struggle with jealousy like some do. Plus, we get along with everyone. The fact that we were invited to another party must mean we left a good impression. So, let's just go with it."

He had a point. We did make friends easily, and given how close we'd become with others in the lifestyle, it was only natural for them to talk about us. Maryann had even given me Debbie's phone number, and I called to confirm our attendance. She remembered us fondly and was happy we would join them at the party.

"So, why the fancy dinner?" Ryan asked with a smirk on his face.

185

"Well," I began, trying to play coy, "I wanted to go to the party, and I wanted to make my husband happy so he would say yes."

Ryan just stared at me before shaking his head and laughing. "What have I created?"

I playfully slapped his arm before walking off as he continued to laugh hysterically.

As I stepped back into the kitchen, I couldn't help but reflect on how much I'd changed in the past year, or even since our first time at the Cove. This lifestyle had brought a new level of excitement and fun into our marriage. We'd been flirting with each other more than ever before. It was like we were experiencing a whole new way to live and appreciate life.

Over the next few days, Ryan and I talked about the upcoming party quite frequently, often engaging in pillow talk late into the night. Our rules had loosened up a bit, and we were both more comfortable with the idea of attending lifestyle events. While we may not have been "party virgins" anymore, there was still so much for us to learn.

We discussed our boundaries and agreed to allow for independent exploration. If one of us found someone we were interested in playing with, we would let the other know beforehand. I made sure to remind Ryan to always use a condom. It wasn't so much about avoiding pregnancy—I'd had my tubes tied after our third child, and Ryan had undergone a vasectomy years ago—but it was important to protect ourselves against any sexually transmitted infections. We had read that STI rates were low among swingers, but we didn't want to take any chances.

"Have you been using condoms?" I asked.

"Yes," he assured me. "And have you been making sure the men you're with are using them?" he asked pointedly.

I hesitated before sheepishly admitting, "At the oyster roast, Jeff was having some trouble staying hard with a condom on. He said it reduces sensation and causes him to go limp, so we took it off to see if it would help."

Ryan looked surprised. "Did it?"

I shook my head slowly. "I don't think so, but then Deedee came in to help out too. I'm not sure if she was successful though."

After a long pause, Ryan spoke up again. "These are just regular couples like you and me. They have the same concerns and lives as us. And since we're both fixed, is using condoms really necessary?"

I pondered his words for a moment. While I didn't particularly enjoy using condoms either, I knew it was important to prioritize our sexual health. "Yes," I finally replied. "Until we get to know someone really well, let's continue using them."

Ryan reluctantly agreed.

On the evening of the party, I made sure to double-check with Ryan that he had condoms with him before we left. He reached into his back pocket and showed me two of them, a confident grin on his face.

"That's optimistic," I replied sarcastically.

"Where are yours?" he asked, raising an eyebrow.

I opened a hidden zipper pocket in my purse, where I had secretly tucked away about six condoms.

Ryan couldn't help but laugh. "Who's calling who optimistic now?"

I rolled my eyes playfully. "Let's just go have fun."

On the drive over to the party, Ryan brought up some fantasies he wanted to fulfill. The biggest priority on his list was having two women at the same time.

"I'm not into women," I reminded him sternly.

He shot me a mischievous grin. "You sure seemed pretty into three of them at the last party."

A blush crept up my cheeks as I remembered that wild night in the hot tub with Maryann, Terra, and Jackie. "Okay, maybe it was exciting in the moment, but it isn't something I actively seek out. Let's just see what happens tonight and have no expectations."

After a few moments of silence, Ryan spoke up again. "That's probably for the best, but at least you know what I want."

As we continued our journey, my mind couldn't help but drift back to that hot tub experience and my first encounter with Deedee. Was it possible that I actually liked women and just never realized it? These confusing thoughts made me question if my conservative upbringing had created a barrier in exploring my true desires. But one thing was for sure—I would be lying if I said I hadn't enjoyed it that night.

Debbie and Mark's home was in a lovely split-level house nestled in a quaint middle-class neighborhood. Basketball hoops dotted the parking lots, and midsize family cars and vans filled the driveways—the quintessential picture of suburban life.

We walked up to the front door and rang the doorbell. Jackie answered, her face lighting up when she saw me. "Ginger!" she exclaimed, pulling me into a warm hug. "And Ryan, my favorite couple," she teased as she gave him a lingering kiss hello.

I couldn't help but watch as Jackie's tongue seemed to explore every inch of Ryan's mouth. A twinge of envy shot through me. A small part of me wanted her to kiss me like that too.

As we made our way inside, I couldn't help but feel dazed by the buzzing energy of the house. The familiar faces in the crowd helped to ground me, and I forced a smile as we made our way into the house. Despite being frequent guests of this lifestyle, both Ryan and I struggled with remembering names. It used to embarrass us, but thankfully, most people here weren't offended.

Jackie promised to give us a tour of the house and led us into the bustling kitchen. There was Debbie, looking radiant as ever.

"Look who I just found!" Jackie exclaimed.

Debbie's face lit up when she saw us. "Oh, I'm so glad you could make it!" She leaned in and gave me a warm embrace before turning to Ryan for a kiss as well.

"Just put your cooler down by the kitchen wall," Debbie instructed us. "Set your fruit tray on the table and mingle. The hot tub is in the back. Have a great time!"

We thanked her for the invite, and Ryan retrieved some drinks from our cooler before we set off to explore the party. We spotted a couple we'd met at the last event, but unfortunately, their names escaped us once again. Determined not to let that stop us from making connections, we approached them with friendly smiles and introduced ourselves again. They were Eddie and Darcy, both about a decade older than us.

Eddie was an average build with graying hair he'd attempted to hide with a comb-over. I didn't judge him for it; it was always about more than physical appearance for me. He seemed like a gregarious person and kept us entertained with his lively conversation. Darcy was tall and slim with an alluring olive complexion. Her outfit—a short skirt paired with a loose-fitting blouse, and no bra—exuded a bold and sexy confidence.

As we chatted, Eddie suddenly suggested, "Since the party is just starting, would you two like to get some playtime in early?"

I shot a quick glance at Ryan, hoping he would read my expression as a firm "no" or "not now." But his confusion was evident and I found myself stuck in an uncomfortable situation. In that moment, I wished I'd spoken up and made it clear that we wanted to get to know people before jumping into bed. But it was too late now, and I didn't want to create any drama by objecting. So, with a sigh, I reluctantly agreed, frustrated at my own lack of assertiveness.

Note to self: Train Ryan to read my nonverbal cues better.

As we ascended the stairs, the anticipation was palpable. The first bedroom door to our left was slightly ajar, and without hesitation, we entered and closed the door behind us. Ryan and Darcy were already entwined on the other side of the large bed, passionately making out and eagerly removing each other's clothing.

Eddie started kissing me, but there wasn't an electric connection like I had with Ryan, or others. Perhaps if we had more time to get to know each other . . .

Eddie wasn't unattractive, but he didn't really flip my switch either. Overall, he was a fun guy, so I decided to relax and enjoy the moment. I kissed him gently at first and let the pace gradually become more passionate. He began to take off my top. I fumbled with his belt and pants, hoping a hard cock would get my engine running. We were all totally nude within a few minutes.

I knelt, took Eddie in my hand, and stroked him. Looking up into his eyes, I wrapped my lips around him, then gradually slid my mouth farther and farther down, my saliva coating his length. I reached around to grab his ass cheeks, allowing him to slowly fuck my mouth. My sexual excitement wasn't very high so early into the party, so I was sort of going through the motions. Fortunately, he was well-groomed, and I quickly realized why so many SLS profiles mentioned grooming preferences.

I peeked over to see Ryan and Darcy on the bed in a sixty-nine position. They both appeared to be pros in that skill.

As Eddie grew rock-hard in my mouth and hands, I couldn't help but feel a sense of satisfaction at the thought of experiencing his package myself.

"Lay back on the bed," he whispered.

I anticipated him sliding inside of me, but I complied. He pushed my legs back, then knelt and slid his tongue over my heat instead. I loved oral too, but I'd just gotten him hard to hurry up and fuck me. But the unexpected pleasure sent shivers down my spine, and I relaxed into the sensation, letting go of any rush or desire to be done with it quickly.

Eddie explored my depths with his talented tongue, eventually adding two fingers inside of me, and slowly thrusted them in and out while expertly tickling my G-spot. Every stroke had my body craving more, aching for release.

I lost track of time as he brought me closer and closer to the edge, until finally I couldn't hold back any longer. In a desperate plea, I begged him to fuck me now. And without hesitation, he stood up and positioned himself between my wide-open legs, ready to claim what I desired.

But as I looked down at him stroking himself to get hard again, panic set in. He wasn't wearing a condom, and in my overwhelmed state, I couldn't even remember where I'd put mine. Desperate for the fulfillment of our desires, I dropped to my knees in front of Eddie and frantically sucked him off to make him hard again. Meanwhile, I rubbed my own sex with one hand, trying to keep myself aroused and ready.

My eyes strayed over to Ryan and Darcy once again, now fully engaged in sex, with a condom securely in place. As I watched them move together with reckless abandon, all I could think was how badly I wanted that same connection with Eddie.

Finally, after what felt like an eternity of sucking and rubbing, Eddie was hard once again. And without further hesitation, or further thought of protection, we both gave into our carnal desires and began to have sex. I wrapped my legs around him, my body practically begging for him to fill me. But despite the physical pleasure, a nagging voice in my mind reminded me of the risks we were taking. And as we lost ourselves in the moment, I couldn't help but feel a sense of unease creeping in, but it was quickly squelched.

"Oh yes," I moaned. I needed it. Although I wasn't as heated up as I was a few minutes ago, his cock was big and thick enough to get me going again. He stretched me out well as he slid deep into me and fucked me hard and fast. Now we were getting somewhere. His prior G-spot stimulation had made me swollen, and he reached the right spots with every thrust.

Within a couple of minutes, I the electricity built inside me, tingling and pulsing through my body. My skin pebbled with goose bumps as the pleasure intensified. Involuntary moans escaped my lips as I arched my back in anticipation.

But just as I was on the brink of climax, he slowed down. Panic rose within me—what was he doing? I tilted my hips, silently pleading for him to continue, but his movements lacked enthusiasm. When I looked up at him, his eyes were closed in concentration.

Suddenly, he pulled out, and I gasped in frustration. How could he lose his erection at such a crucial moment? Disappointed, I slid off the bed once again and tried to arouse him with my mouth. But it was like trying to light a fire with an ice cube—he just wouldn't get hard again.

He apologized profusely, but it did little to comfort me. As he kept insisting this had never happened before, doubts crept into my mind. Was there something wrong with me? First Jeff, now Eddie—both unable to perform. Was it all because of me?

In the midst of my internal turmoil, Darcy moaned loudly from her second orgasm. But here I was, unable to get Eddie hard again. Defeated and dejected, I went up to kiss him, and he apologized once more. I forced an accepting grin and tried to hide my disappointment.

Meanwhile, Ryan and Darcy were still going at it on the other side of the room. When Ryan caught sight of my expression, he whispered something in Darcy's ear, and they both joined us on the bed.

"Hey, guys," Darcy said with a mischievous glint in her eye. "Why don't we turn up the heat a little bit?"

She gently pried open my legs and placed her mouth on my very wet sex. Her deliberate movements and expert attention to my most sensitive areas sent waves of pleasure through me. It was a revelation to experience how well women knew how to orally please other women. I loved men, but there was something completely different about the way a woman touched and tasted.

Ryan knelt beside me, his hard cock pushing against my lips. Without hesitation, I took him in, tasting Darcy on him from their previous encounter. Part of me wanted to stop and protest, but another part couldn't resist my desire for her taste. As I pleasured him with my mouth, I reached over and stroked Eddie with my hand. He wasn't responding much, but at this point, it didn't matter—I was close to climaxing again.

Darcy continued her delicious torment on me, her tongue working magic on my clit while she delicately fingered me. My body churned and writhed as I neared nirvana once again.

"I'm almost there," I gasped, urging them all to keep going. And with one final thrust of Ryan's hips and a gentle caress from Darcy's fingers, I reached the pinnacle of ecstasy once again.

The rough, calloused texture of a man's hand rubbed against my swollen clit, sending sparks coursing through me. I glanced down and saw Darcy was still between my legs, but my focus was on the intense sensations building inside me. I didn't care who was doing what. I just wanted to reach the peak of ecstasy.

"Come for me, baby," Ryan whispered huskily in my ear. And with those words, my body tensed and then exploded in a wave of pure bliss. My head fell back and I cried out as the orgasm washed over me in powerful waves.

Darcy crawled closer, her lips finding mine in a gentle kiss. The taste of myself lingered on her lips, driving me wild with desire.

I tangled my fingers in her hair and pulled her closer, deepening the kiss and showing her my gratitude with my tongue. There was something undeniably erotic about the way two women could pleasure each other, something that men could never replicate. And as I tasted my own essence on her lips, I thought about how good it must have felt for her too.

A movement caught my attention, and I opened my eyes to see Darcy release herself from our embrace and gasp with pleasure. My gaze shifted Ryan as he thrust into her from behind, his hands gripping her hips. Darcy leaned down to continue kissing me while Ryan's movements became more urgent and forceful. She broke the kiss and closed her eyes as she reached her own climax. After a moment of release, she lay down next to me.

Ryan's hands trailed down to my legs, and he pulled me closer to the edge of the bed. He pushed my legs back and declared, "Now it's your turn."

With one swift motion, he removed his condom and plunged into me, filling me completely as Eddie and Darcy caressed my breasts. My body had barely recovered from the previous orgasm and I was already on fire again, my moans of pleasure growing louder with each thrust.

Darcy must have really worked Ryan up, because within minutes, his face turned red and his whole body tensed as he growled, "I'm coming!"

I wrapped my legs tightly around his waist, pulling him closer as his climax triggered another powerful orgasm within me. I cried out so loudly that I was sure the neighbors could hear.

When he finally pulled out and collapsed next to me, I couldn't stop trembling from the intensity of my release. Eddie seemed a bit uninterested in the whole experience, and I felt a twinge of guilt. But then I remembered how they all had made sure to make me feel good, which dissipated my guilty feelings.

"Maybe we should head back down to the party," Darcy suggested.

Ryan chuckled. "I don't know about you guys, but for me, the real party was up here."

We all laughed and got dressed before heading downstairs.

Amid the chatter and music of the party, Jackie's voice rang out like a bell. "Ginger, I love what you've done with your hair!"

As all eyes turned toward us, my face flushed with embarrassment.

Ryan smirked at me and chuckled, his gaze taking in my new hairstyle. "You've got that just-been-fucked look, sweetie."

I gave Jackie a warm hug and kiss in response to her compliment.

She then turned to Ryan. "Why doesn't your beautiful wife have a drink in her hand?"

I laughed. "I'm actually going to freshen up in the bathroom, but I'll take a rum and coke when I get back."

I made my way through the crowded room, and Ryan had my drink ready for me by the time I returned.

As Jackie and I sipped our drinks, we caught up on each other's lives. She was someone who radiated positive energy, her beauty shining from within. Always wearing a bright smile on her face, she had a knack for bringing happiness to anyone around her. It was enjoyable to be around her, and if I could choose a woman to experiment with, it would definitely be her.

We laughed at some funny stories we'd overheard before Jackie invited me to join her in the hot tub.

"Just remember," she teased. "You can't scream outside like you did upstairs."

We both giggled at the memory before heading outside.

"I'll try to control myself," I replied flirtatiously, leaning into Jackie's arm. "But you turn me on so much, I can't promise anything."

My desires toward women had been growing ever since that first encounter with Deedee—and especially tonight, after Ryan had blatantly pointed it out during our drive over. Jackie was probably the first woman I truly desired.

As we stepped outside, I saw Ryan talking to a new person—an attractive, smiling woman around thirty-five years old with long, jet-black hair and bib overalls with one side unbuckled. He introduced her as Janet, and she'd

198

clearly captivated him. I told him I was going to join Jackie in the hot tub.

"Maybe we'll join you in a little while," Janet said with a playful smile.

"That would be great," I replied before kissing Ryan. "Have fun," I whispered with a wink before walking toward the inviting bubbles of the hot tub, where Jackie was already undressing.

There were four others in the hot tub—two men and two women. I recognized Maryann, but the other three were strangers to me. Feeling braver than last time, I didn't need any encouragement to remove my clothes. As I stepped into the bubbling spa, the men stood up with outstretched hands to help me in.

Smiling gratefully, I eased myself into the water. "Such gentlemen," I commented playfully. "But just so you know, I don't have sex with strangers." My eyes met Ryan's across the crowded yard and couldn't resist adding, "So, why don't you introduce yourselves, and maybe we can get to know each other?"

Everyone laughed at my boldness, and the men introduced themselves as Brian and Darren, and the other woman in the hot tub was named Emma. Maryann came over to give me a warm kiss.

"I know Maryann," I said. "Are any of you three together?"

Emma said, "Darren and I are married, and we just met Brian a few minutes ago."

"My wife, Janet, is in the house," Brian said. "She might come out here later."

"I just met Janet, actually," I said. "She was talking to my husband, Ryan."

"If I know my wife, they won't be talking for long," Brian replied.

I laughed. "Well, then she found the right guy. He's always ready to go."

We all talked for a while, laughing about fun and sexy experiences. Then Jackie said, "Hmmm. We have two attractive men and four attractive women in a hot tub without clothes on. Why are we just talking?"

"I think the men should sit on the edge of the hot tub while we have our way with them," Maryann said.

Brian, of course, replied, "I think that's a great idea."

We laughed as they got up and sat on the edge of the spa. I wandered over to Emma and Darren while Jackie drifted toward Brian and Maryann.

Emma's hand wrapped around Darren's shaft, her fingers gliding up and down the length of it with practiced ease. She then offered it to me, holding it like a delicate gift for me to indulge in.

I leaned forward, meeting Emma's lips in a gentle kiss before looking up at Darren as I took him into my mouth. He gasped in pleasure and Emma whispered, "I love watching him get pleased by another woman."

I paused for a moment and replied, "Well, then I hope I don't disappoint either of you."

Darren moaned in response, his eyes locked on mine.

I pulled back and kissed him deeply while Emma worked her magic on his cock. My hand reached behind his head to pull him closer as our tongues danced together. Then I traced the outline of his lips with my tongue before returning to kiss Emma. Together, we focused on giving Darren the ultimate pleasure. Our mouths moved in perfect unison along his length, tilting our heads to avoid getting in each other's way.

As our tongues swirled around the tip of his hard cock, we occasionally stopped to share a passionate kiss between ourselves. Darren's legs trembled, and we knew he was about to climax. And, sure enough, he cried out, "Oh God, I'm coming!"

But we didn't stop pleasuring him as he unleashed warm streams of cum onto both of our lips and cheeks like a small fountain. While Emma stroked him to ensure he was completely spent, I gently massaged his balls.

Once he was finished, Emma placed her hands on my cheeks and we kissed again. She playfully licked away Darren's seed from my face before we resumed making out, all while stealing glances at him and smiling mischievously.

"I've never done that before," I admitted shyly. "But it was incredibly hot." Ryan would never believe I was capable of such a daring act.

Emma and I continued to kiss but soon noticed that Jackie and Maryann were still busy with Brian. Without hesitation, I motioned for Emma to join me as we swam behind Jackie and Maryann. Our hands roamed over their bodies as we kissed their necks and reached around to grab their breasts. They eagerly turned around to kiss us back.

Laughing, Emma apologized, "Sorry for interrupting."

But Brian assured us, "No, please continue. I'm enjoying this too."

Exchanging sly grins, Jackie and I resumed our passionate kissing while Emma and Maryann did the same.

And when Ryan and Janet approached us, asking if there was room for two more, Jackie enthusiastically replied, "Absolutely!"

The atmosphere was filled with laughter and playful banter as we all enjoyed each other's company.

"Is that Darren I taste on your lips?" Jackie teased me.

I glanced over at Darren, who blushed and raised his beer in response. We all laughed before diving back into kissing. But there was something special about my connection with Jackie that I couldn't explain.

Ryan

I held out my hand for Janet as she stepped into the hot tub, her eyes twinkling with mischief. I followed her, the water's heat immediately soothing my tense muscles.

202

Janet and I had been getting to know each other, and I found myself drawn to her. She was stunning, a bit curvier than my usual type, but her personality was magnetic. Her sexuality radiated through every touch and kiss, and I craved more.

Just as we were about to sit in the spa, Jackie planted a kiss on Janet's lips. They seemed familiar with each other.

"I hope my husband has been taking care of you ladies," Janet smiled.

Brian grinned. "We've been having a great time so far."

I was about to sink into the steaming water when Janet grabbed my arm. "Oh, no you don't. There's something I've been wanting to do for the past half an hour."

She knelt in the water, taking me by surprise as she engulfed my soft cock in her mouth. Her warm mouth and hunger sparked an immediate reaction.

Brian laughed. "Now that's the Janet I know."

She stuck her tongue out at him. "Leave me alone, I'm busy."

We all laughed as she worked my cock with fervor, the audience adding an extra thrill. In no time, I was rock-hard.

Vigorously stroking my shaft, she said, "This is what I was hoping for."

She pushed her mouth onto my cock, trying to fit it down her throat, gagging on the tip. I marveled at her determination, glancing over at Ginger, whose mouth hung open in amazement.

Jackie knelt beside Janet. "I definitely remember this cock. Can I share?"

Now I stood in the middle of the hot tub, two women eagerly enjoying my cock while others watched. I looked at Ginger, who smiled and winked, as she sat with Darren, his hands on her and Emma's breasts.

Janet and Jackie kissed each other intermittently, their eyes locking with mine, driving me wild with lust. Then Janet told me to sit down. She climbed onto my lap, kissing me deeply while grinding against my cock.

"I have other talents too," she whispered with a sly grin, her eyes dark with anticipation.

She slid off my lap, grabbing my shaft before her head disappeared underwater. I felt her lips wrap around my cock. She was sucking me underwater. When she surfaced for air, everyone clapped. She laughed and went back under.

I made eye contact with Ginger, who shook her head, laughing. "Don't ever expect that from me."

Janet emerged, crawling back onto my lap. She positioned herself so that my shaft split her swollen lips, teasing me without letting me in. We made out, her body rubbing against my aching dick.

"I want to be inside you so badly," I moaned.

She smiled and whispered, "What I learned from ten years in the medical field is, don't fuck in hot tubs."

I didn't quite understand, but she sealed her lips to mine again, continuing to grind against me, pushing me to the edge of desire.

"Would you like to fuck me upstairs?" Janet's voice, dripping with desire, cut through the humid air.

I met her gaze, an excited smirk curling my lips. "Absolutely."

She drifted over to Ginger, her movements fluid and purposeful. "Do you mind if I take your husband upstairs and have my way with him?"

Ginger glanced at me, a playful spark in her eyes. "Sweetie, have as much fun with him as you like."

Janet leaned over to kiss Ginger softly, then stood up and reached for my hand. I hadn't expected Ginger's quick acceptance. She must have felt very comfortable. I was glad we were acclimating to this lifestyle so well, without any hint of jealousy.

Janet and I dried off and wrapped our towels around ourselves before heading upstairs.

"Should we take our clothes?" I asked.

"They'll be there when we come back." She held her towel with one hand and linked her other arm with mine. "Show me the way."

We walked into the house, now filled with about thirty guests. Conversations paused as we walked in, wearing nothing but towels. Janet didn't seem to notice, so we made our way upstairs, spotting an open room.

The towels dropped before we'd even crossed the threshold. Janet's kiss set me on fire, our mutual hunger igniting a fervor that only raw chemistry could create. We stumbled into the room, making out aggressively, lightly biting each other's lips and caressing each other's bodies. She gasped as I grabbed a fistful of her hair at the base of her skull and tilted her head to the side, exposing her beautiful neck. I kissed and lightly bit her neck just under her hairline, making her moan and squirm in my grip. I held her hair tightly, which seemed to turn her on even more.

When I released her, she pushed me back onto the bed and practically pounced on me. She kissed my neck and throat, then trailed her lips and tongue down my chest to my nipples. She sucked one, then the other before lightly biting down. I jumped, unsure whether I liked the sensation. She giggled, drifting farther down until she had my cock in her hand. Looking up into my eyes, she stroked me, swirling her tongue around the tip, kissing it, and licking the sides before lunging her throat down my shaft. I gasped at the sudden sensation. She fucked my cock with her mouth, her hunger and pride in the act turning me on even more.

She took a condom from the nightstand, unwrapped it, and placed it in her mouth. I watched in awe as she put her mouth on the tip of my cock and pushed the condom down with her lips. Yet another one of her talents. She crawled up my body and straddled my hips, our eyes locked as she slowly lowered herself down.

I tore my gaze away to witness the incredible sight of my dick stretching her open. When I looked up again, her face twisted with both pain and pleasure. Her lips parted and her breathing quickened as she inched her way down.

206

She lifted herself up and back down, gyrating her hips in gentle circles before picking up the pace. I groaned, gritting my teeth. She was so wet, her pussy sliding easily up and down my cock. She leaned back a bit, shifting her legs forward to fuck me while squatting over me, giving me the most incredible show as her pussy swallowed my cock over and over.

"You like watching your cock slide into me?" she asked, her voice husky.

My eyes locked onto hers again. At that moment, I could have exploded, but our earlier encounter had given me more control. "I like it a lot."

She fucked me with an intense rhythm, and I reached up, massaging her breasts. I pinched her nipples, eliciting a gasp. She dug her nails into my neck, and I pinched harder in response. Her nails bit into my skin deeper, and I retaliated with more pressure on her nipples until she released her grip, laughing.

"Okay, enough." She rolled off me, spreading her legs wide in a *V*, her pussy lips parted, her entrance glistening. I was nearly drunk with lust. "I want you to fuck me really hard and fast."

How could I refuse? I slid into her swollen, wet pussy, starting slowly but firmly. Her breathing grew ragged, and the sight of her heaving breasts spurred me on. I increased my pace, her moans escalating in pitch.

Then it happened. She came hard, squirting all over me. The spray of her orgasm coated my cock and balls, running down my legs. It was like nothing I'd ever felt.

"Sorry. I should have told you I squirt a lot when I get really excited."

I laughed. "I'm just glad the bed isn't mine."

Janet sat up, making me slide out of her. She grabbed a towel from the nightstand and knelt on the edge of the bed, her ass in the air, her torso pressed against the mattress. "I want you to fuck me hard and pull my hair until I come."

Taking direction from a woman in rough sex was new for me, but I aimed to please. I slid back into her drenched pussy, gripping her hair, and fucked her harder. She came quickly and repeatedly, her nectar running down my legs, splashing between us.

"Choke me," she demanded.

I hesitated. "What?"

"Choke me. Put your hand on my throat."

I reached around, my hand trembling as I wrapped it around her throat. She pushed back against me, thrusting harder.

"Choke me harder," she panted.

I complied, adding pressure without hurting her. An animalistic surge rippled through me. I gripped her throat and fucked her with abandon, my orgasm hitting me like a freight train. I howled, my body shuddering, cum pouring from me in waves. I held her throat until the pulsating lessened, then released her. I was so overwhelmed I hadn't noticed if she came with me.

Janet turned, laughing. "That was fun. We definitely need to meet you two again."

"Wow. I've never met anyone like you before."

We kissed for a few minutes before she suggested we head back to the party. My body and mind were euphoric, basking in the aftermath of our electrifying sex. There were no demands for cuddling or emotional bonding. It was just a simple, incredible encounter.

We wrapped ourselves in towels and headed downstairs, where Brian and Ginger were talking in the kitchen, also in towels. We kissed our respective spouses, and then Janet gave Ginger a long, soft kiss.

"Thank you," Janet said. "I hope we can get your number before we leave."

Ginger

After Janet thanked me for letting Ryan play with her, I nodded. "You're welcome. Did he do well?"

She giggled, sounding a bit guilty, "Oh, he did very well."

"We should exchange numbers," I suggested.

Ryan's grin told me all I needed to know—they'd clearly hit it off. Sadly, I couldn't say the same about my evening. Our earlier encounter had been salvaged, but it lacked the intensity I craved. I had hoped Brian would invite me upstairs, but he never did.

I struggled to ask for what I wanted. What was wrong with me? I couldn't seem to voice my desires, or refuse when needed. Was it a fear of rejection? Plain shyness? I didn't know. I felt a whirlwind of emotions about our first experience playing separately. I was glad Ryan had an amazing time, but damn it, I craved more earth-shattering fun too.

We mingled with other couples for about thirty minutes. One guy, a natural storyteller, recounted hilarious lifestyle events from his past. His stories seemed unreal, but as newcomers, we were in awe.

One tale involved a couple he and his wife had been with. They'd started with oral and fingering, but the woman wanted more. She kept asking for more fingers, until he ended up with half his arm inside her. When he pulled out, she asked if he was going to fuck her. His response was, "Hell, I've got nothing left that you would feel after that."

The room erupted in laughter, tears streaming down some people's faces.

As we laughed, commotion outside drew our attention. Everyone turned toward the open sliding glass door. Mark and Debbie's dog had escaped. The small black lab darted into the house, pausing in the kitchen with excitement, tongue hanging out, tail wagging. The dog scanned the room, deciding where to go next.

Suddenly, he bolted down the hallway. Those of us with a view saw an unforgettable scene. At the end of the hall, Janet was on her knees, sucking on Kurt. In a split-second, the dog lunged, licking Janet's face and inadvertently getting a bit of Kurt too.

210

It happened so fast that neither of them reacted immediately. Kurt, lost in pleasure, didn't notice the dog at first. Then he jolted, cupping himself with both hands as the dog kept licking. Kurt spun around, facing the wall. The onlookers burst into hysterical laughter, growing louder as the dog started licking Kurt's ass. Janet, laughing, grabbed the dog by the collar and pulled him back. If someone had told me this story, I wouldn't have believed it.

The dog backed off, panting and wagging his tail. Debbie lunged forward, grabbed the dog by the collar, and yanked him away from Janet.

"I'm so sorry!" she said, frantic. She hustled the dog outside, leaving an awkward silence in her wake.

The rest of the night blurred by. After midnight, I hit my socializing limit. Tipsy and exhausted, I turned to Ryan. "Can we go home?" I asked, my voice heavy with fatigue.

As we got our coats, I struggled to stand, my legs unsteady. I leaned my butt against the living room wall, trying to regain my balance.

While I finished dressing, Jackie approached, wrapped in a towel. "Leaving without saying goodbye?" she teased, her eyes glinting with mischief.

She leaned in for a quick kiss. The brief contact reignited a fire inside me. I grabbed the top of her towel as she stepped back. "You're not getting away that easy," I said, my voice low.

Our lips met again in a passionate kiss. I'd never wanted a woman like this before, but in that moment,

211

nothing existed except Jackie's lips on mine and our tongues dancing together. She slipped her hand into my blouse, cupping my breasts. I responded in kind, her towel dropping to the floor. Her nipples hardened under my touch as I caressed her.

We kissed for what felt like minutes. When we finally pulled away, I realized everyone was staring at us.

"What's everyone looking at? Can't two friends kiss?" I asked, my cheeks burning.

"Wow," Ryan murmured, his voice barely audible.

"Did you like that, baby?" I asked, a playful smile tugging at my lips.

He nodded, and I felt a surge of satisfaction. I loved that I could still surprise him.

As we reached for our cooler, an attractive young woman of about thirty approached us. "Hi, I'm Kathy," she said, extending her hand.

I shook her hand, and Ryan gave her a hug. She introduced her boyfriend, Brad, who looked even younger than Kathy. He seemed shy, almost nervous. We apologized, explaining we were about to leave for the night, but Kathy was persistent.

"I just wanted to make sure you got our invitation for a house party in a few months," she said, smiling warmly.

I didn't know her, but Ryan looked intrigued. The party was on a Saturday, and we had no plans, but I wasn't ready to commit.

"We'll have to check our schedule and get back to you," I said, trying to sound noncommittal.

Kathy handed us her SLS profile screen name and her phone number. "I'd like people who enjoy playing, and you two seem like a fun couple," she said, her eyes twinkling with invitation.

Ryan's excitement was palpable.

"Thanks for the invite. We'll see what's going on and let you know," I said, trying to keep us grounded.

Ryan smiled and hugged Kathy again. "We'll try to make it."

We didn't know Kathy or her young boyfriend, and yet Ryan was already implying we'd attend. I shook my head, bemused.

We made our rounds, kissing everyone goodnight and exchanging phone numbers with Brian, Janet, Darren, and Emma. Just as we were about to leave, Debbie came running up, waving a card.

"Wait, wait!" she called out excitedly.

Mark approached Debbie from behind. "We want to invite you to our wedding," she said, handing me the card.

Ryan and I exchanged glances as I opened the invitation. It really was a wedding invite. The card featured a silhouette of a man in a top hat with his arm around a woman in a corset, short skirt, and top hat, with a large red heart behind them.

"You two are a lot of fun," Debbie said. "We'd love for you to come. It's a Moulin Rouge theme, and we're encouraging the women to dress up, but you don't have to."

Tears welled up in my eyes. Debbie noticed immediately. "Sweetie, what's the matter?"

I wiped my eyes and hugged her. "We're so new to all of this, and I feel so honored to be invited to your wedding."

"Oh, Ginger, you two are so very welcome. We love having you as friends."

I wiped more tears from my eyes and looked at the card again. "Oh, it's in two weeks?"

"Yes, can you make it? We have a block of rooms reserved at the hotel."

I looked up at Ryan. He had wanted to commit to a party with people we didn't know without discussing it with me privately first, so I thought I'd commit to people we did know. "Sure, we can make it," I said.

We hugged again and headed home. On the way, I must have been deep in thought because Ryan asked, "Is something wrong?"

I looked at him, grabbed his hand, and said, "I'm fine. I just didn't have as much fun this evening as you did."

"Oh, sweetie, I'm sorry. I thought you were doing well in the spa."

"I thought so too, but when I tried to work on Darren again, he said he was spent for the night. I hung out with Brian for a little while, but all he did was talk, and he

214

wouldn't ask me to play. Then earlier with Eddie and Darcy . . . I just didn't have the best evening." I continued, "I'm glad you had a great time. Janet seemed like a lot of fun."

He glanced at me. "You have no idea. She really electrified me."

I laughed. "Oh, really! I've never heard you say that before. She isn't quite who I would expect you to play with. She is pretty, but heavier than who you're usually interested in."

He nodded. "When she approached me, I didn't think I would be interested either, but she's funny and has a certain dominant-submissive side that I find really exciting."

I was surprised but also elated, since Janet provided something for him that I didn't enjoy. I wanted Ryan to have all the extra fun that I'm not comfortable with, and for him to enjoy the women he finds captivating, but I was also happy to have him return to me at the end of the evening.

"What do you think about the wedding?" he asked.

I grabbed the invitation to look at it, laughing softly. "I guess we *are* definitely on the list."

Ryan smiled and looked at me. "I'm curious what a swinger Moulin Rouge-themed wedding would be like, but I'm sure it'll be fun."

When we got home, we were both exhausted. We cleaned up and went straight to bed. Ryan snuggled up behind me and put his arm around me.

"I love you, sweetie," he said.

Ending our adventurous evenings like this, recharging in each other's arms, I knew our love and marriage were strong enough for us to have fun with new friends without it getting between us. We could have all the fun we wanted at parties, but we would always end the night together. I snuggled into his embrace.

"I love you too," I whispered back.

Chapter 18: Moulin Rouge Wedding

Ginger

The wedding ceremony started at 4:00 p.m. on a small lakeside beach about twenty miles away. Debbie told us to dress casually for the ceremony and change at the hotel for the reception, which started at six. I packed a pretty purple-and-black corset, a short black miniskirt I'd bought at an adult toy store, and a pair of black strappy heels that Ryan loved on me. Ryan dressed simply in a nice button-down linen shirt and black slacks for both events.

We arrived at the ceremony location fifteen minutes early and spotted several familiar faces. Naturally, we gravitated toward socializing with our lifestyle friends. Kurt and Maryann were there, and Maryann mentioned that the family would attend only the ceremony, so we needed to keep things PG until later.

When Mark and his groomsmen showed up, we took our seats. The wedding march played from a portable stereo somewhere, and soon, Debbie appeared for her walk down the aisle. All jaws dropped. She wore a white corset that showcased her impressive breasts, and what looked like a short white skirt with a mesh-like train. All eyes were on her gorgeous legs as she walked down the aisle.

I discreetly elbowed Ryan. "Wipe off that drool."

He smiled, put his arm around me, and we watched the rest of the wedding. It proceeded like any other, with a minister, vows, and a kiss, and then the newlyweds walked down the aisle. I had never seen a wedding dress so revealing and sexy. I couldn't wait to see what Debbie would wear to the reception.

We drove to the hotel where the reception was being held, and checked into our room. Since we still had an hour before the reception started, we headed down to the bar. Kurt and Maryann joined us.

"Did you know what her dress was going to look like?" I asked.

Maryann laughed. "I went with her and Jackie to find it."

"I can't wait to see what she wears to the reception," Ryan said.

Kurt widened his eyes and nodded.

"She just takes her train off, and she's ready to party," Maryann said. "I'm so glad they invited you. At their party a couple of weeks ago, I suggested for Debbie to invite you. I'm glad she did."

"I can't believe the friendships we've created in this lifestyle," I said, tears gathering in my eyes. "It's so much more than we ever dreamed of."

Maryann reached out to hug me. "Aw, you're a great friend too. Ryan, don't just stand there, get your wife a tissue."

Kurt reached around Maryann and me. "Aw, group hug. We should continue this upstairs in our room."

Maryann slapped Kurt on the arm, and we all laughed.

I took the tissue Ryan handed me and wiped my eyes. "Well, I need to go up and get ready."

I received a text from Kurt: He and Maryann were heading down to the reception area. I quickly replied, "We'll be there shortly."

"Are we ready?" I asked Ryan, glancing over him.

He grinned, eyes lingering on the choker around my neck. "You look amazing," he said and leaned in to kiss my neck. His hands slid along my legs and up my skirt, sending shivers down my spine.

I giggled, pulling away. "Let's go enjoy the reception. And FYI, this is a choker, not a collar, so no leash jokes." I was never into the BDSM scene. Ryan has always wanted to put a leash on me, and even though I knew it was for play, I never liked it.

Ryan laughed, giving me a playful slap on the ass. "For now."

The hotel ballroom, where the reception was held, dazzled with rich colors, gold accents, high ceilings, and large crystal chandeliers. We made our way to the bar, where Kurt and Maryann found us. Maryann's eyes lit up at my outfit, her own cream-colored skirt and blue corset mirroring mine.

Kurt traced a finger along my neck and grinned. "Nice touch."

I nodded toward Ryan. "His idea. I don't usually wear this kind of thing."

Kurt's eyes twinkled mischievously. "It'll go well with that prop over there." He pointed to a large wooden cross against the opposite wall, the kind I'd seen in adult toy stores. "Ever seen anyone on a St. Andrew's cross?"

Ryan's smile widened. "I like how you think."

I blushed, turning back to them. "Get those ideas right out of your minds if you want any chance with me tonight."

Both men mimed zipping their lips, making me laugh.

We wandered around the ballroom, taking in the various activities. Near the wooden cross, a partitioned area featured mattresses on the floor. Ryan ran his hands over the wood, picking up a wrist shackle from the top post. He crooked a finger at me, motioning for me to come closer. I smiled and shook my head, walking away. In his dreams.

Kurt and Maryann caught up as I approached the refreshment tables. An ice sculpture of a naked woman on her hands and knees dominated the display. You could pour a shot into her mouth, and it would weave through the ice to chill before reaching your mouth, conveniently placed under the statue's pussy making the recipient place their mouth on her icy mound to accept the drink.

"You'll have an easier time getting me to take a shot from this than get on that cross," I said to Ryan.

Kurt dashed off, returning moments later with a glass of tequila.

I laughed. "Don't pour all of it. I can't swallow that much." I winked at both men, making them smile.

220

Leaning back, I placed my mouth on the ice between the sculpture's thighs. Kurt poured the shot, and a moment later, the chilled tequila flowed into my mouth. I drank it, wiping away the drops that trickled down my cheek.

"My turn," Maryann said eagerly. She positioned herself as I had, and this time, Ryan poured the tequila. We watched the liquid trace its path through the ice woman's body and into Maryann's mouth.

Lifting her head, she laughed. "This is fun."

Jackie approached, her voice carrying over the crowd. "Here are my gorgeous friends!" She grinned at Maryann. "You've never sucked my pussy that well before."

Maryann retorted, "Well, you've never orgasmed tequila either."

We laughed so hard that tears streamed down my face.

The music blasted, thumping through my veins, and people swarmed the dance floor. Their outfits nailed the Moulin Rouge theme, but with a provocative twist—more skin than I'd ever seen in one place.

When Debbie and Mark arrived, the room erupted in applause and wild cheers. Debbie still wore her wedding dress, though the train was gone, just as Maryann had predicted. I'd never imagined a wedding dress like hers— elegant yet undeniably sexy.

We danced to the pulsating beats, watching people take shots at the ice sculpture. The wooden cross and play area remained untouched for now.

As the night progressed, we switched dance partners, moving fluidly between groups. I was dancing with Jackie when she suddenly grabbed my hips and spun me around.

"Look, they're using the cross," Jackie said.

A man was securing a nude woman to the cross with leather cuffs around her wrists and ankles.

"Let's go see," Jackie urged, eyes sparkling with excitement.

We edged closer, captivated. The man, now shirtless, revealed a body chiseled to perfection, his muscles highlighted under the dim lights.

Maryann leaned in and whispered, "I'd let him whip me if he'd fuck me afterward."

I laughed, shaking my head at her boldness.

The man picked up some type of black leather hilt with leather straps dangling ominously. Jackie whispered, "That's a flogger," as if reading my thoughts.

I watched, entranced. The woman, short and thirty-something with long brunette hair, stood vulnerably against the cross. The man teased her skin with the flogger's ends before he stepped back and struck her breast with a hard, precise motion.

My hand flew to my mouth, a gasp escaping my lips.

The man's eyes met mine, a predatory grin curling his lips. "Would you like to go next?"

I shook my head frantically, backing into Ryan. The man resumed, striking her several more times before soothing her skin with gentle caresses. She cried out with each strike, but her face softened blissfully under his touch.

Ryan's pleading eyes met mine. I firmly said, "Absolutely not!"

Jackie nudged Ryan, her voice teasing. "I bet you'd like to try it."

"Oh, I can't do that to him," I protested, horrified.

Jackie's smile turned wicked. "I'll do it."

Ryan's beam widened.

I stepped aside, surrendering. "Go for it."

Jackie placed one hand on his arm, the other on his chest. "What do you say, Ryan? Care to let me flog you?"

He glanced at me. I shrugged, indifferent. "Are you and I going behind the screened wall afterward?" he asked Jackie.

She grinned. "Absolutely."

"Okay, let's do it."

Ryan

Jackie helped me strip down, and soon I stood naked in the dimly lit hotel ballroom. A growing crowd gathered, their eyes fixed on me. Jackie turned me to face the St. Andrew's cross, securing my wrists and ankles to it. Her

223

fingers traced a delicate path down my back, over my ass, and along my legs. They wandered back up between my thighs, lightly caressing my balls.

Jackie sauntered to a table laden with instruments. "What shall we start with?" Her voice took on a menacing edge.

I craned my neck, catching a glimpse of the ominous tools. She picked up a coiled bullwhip.

"Oh my God, no!" Ginger's voice pierced the air.

Jackie brought the whip to my cheek and shoulder, caressing me with its coiled form. "Is this too much for you?" she asked.

I smiled, nerves crackling through me. "It might be. This is my first time doing anything like this."

Jackie stepped back, her eyes gleaming. "A virgin? I love virgins."

She replaced the whip and selected a large wooden paddle. Bringing it close, she glided it down my back, between my buttocks, and along my thigh. Then she traced back up, rubbing it gently on my balls and cock.

I tried to brace myself for what was coming, her soft touches a deceptive comfort.

Crack!

The sound hit my ears just before the pain seared through my ass. I jumped against the restraints.

Jackie's hand soothed the sore spot. "Too hard?" she whispered.

"Any harder, and I might not be able to handle it," I admitted.

She rubbed my ass, her fingers slipping between my legs to stroke my shaft. I got lost in the sensation of her touch, but then—

Crack!

The pain sliced through me again, sharper this time. I couldn't hold back a cry. "Whoa! Not sure I can take that again."

Jackie's hand caressed my ass, her lips kissing the tender skin. She stroked my balls and cock, her mouth closing around the head. I tried to look down, but my restraints held me firm. My body buzzed with confused sensations, pain mingling with pleasure.

She reached for a flogger. Bringing it close enough for me to see, she glided it down my body, the handle teasing my balls and sliding between my ass cheeks.

"You know, with a little lube . . ." Her voice trailed off suggestively.

"Let's not go there," I interjected quickly.

She giggled, and then the leather straps of the flogger slapped against my back, the rhythmic strikes almost calming. But then—

Crack!

The pain returned, biting into my skin. Another strike followed, and another, forming a cruel X pattern. Each blow drew gasps from me, my muscles tensing in anticipation.

Jackie's warm hand soothed my back, her lips kissing my shoulders. "Was that okay?" she whispered.

"Much better than the paddle," I managed.

She grinned. "Good."

She stepped back, and I braced for another strike. Instead, her hand found its way between my legs again, massaging my balls as she kissed my back. I tensed, waiting. The moment I exhaled, she struck four times in quick succession, each blow landing with precision. The fourth one left me trembling.

Jackie set the flogger down and approached. "How was your first experience?"

"Exhilarating," I breathed.

She smiled, unfastening the restraints. "Great. Now, if you're still interested, we can go behind the screened area, and I'll give you your reward for being such a good boy."

Anticipation surged through me, quickening my breath.

Ginger approached, her eyes wide. "I can't believe you did that, and in front of so many people."

I glanced around, stunned to see a crowd of about fifty watching. Embarrassment flushed my cheeks as I stood there, naked and partially erect. But Jackie's hand in mine dissolved the feeling.

Jackie wrapped her other arm around Ginger. "I was going to give Ryan a treat behind the curtain for being so good. Want to join us?"

226

Ginger smiled but shook her head. "No thanks, sweetie. This is a bit too open for me, but enjoy him. I'm sure he'll enjoy you."

She kissed Jackie, then me. "I'll be with Kurt and Maryann. Have fun."

As Ginger walked away, Jackie said, "I hope you know how wonderful your wife is."

I leaned into Jackie, grabbing her ass. "I sure do. Now, let's get that reward."

We slipped behind the loose curtain of the makeshift enclosure, just cloth dividers on metal frames. Inside were two beds on the floor with sheets and a few random pillows.

Jackie faced me, arms around my neck, and kissed me softly. "You have me. Now, how do you want me?" she whispered.

I stared at her, momentarily stumped. I'd wanted Jackie since that first time in the hot tub, and now that I had her, I felt lost. I tried to recover. "I want you naked."

She grinned and stepped back. I mentally kicked myself for not having a better answer. She wanted me to take charge, but I was nervous. I'd always been confident, but Jackie's friendship with Ginger complicated things. Maybe I was overthinking.

Jackie's voice broke my thoughts. "Can I leave my stockings on?"

I gazed at what she wore—heels, stockings, and a garter. Her perfect figure ignited a fierce desire in me. I closed the distance and kissed her fiercely.

My hands roamed her body as hers explored mine. She whispered in my ear, "Take me, use me as you like."

Her words sent a jolt through me, adrenaline surging. I remembered Janet at the house party and decided to channel that experience. Grabbing Jackie's hair, I pulled her head to the side. She gasped, smiling as I kissed and nibbled her neck.

"Yes, that's it. Take me, use me as you want. My entire body is for you," she panted.

Her words fueled my confidence. "Get on your knees," I commanded.

She complied, placing her hands behind her back, looking up at me with sultry eyes.

"Open your mouth," I said.

She did, and I slid my cock into her mouth. She kept her eyes on mine, her mouth open wide.

I began thrusting into her throat. She gagged, eyes watering, but stayed put, taking everything I gave. Then she grabbed my shaft and devoured me with her mouth while aggressively stroking me with her hand, spitting saliva on my cock for lube. She sucked, ran her lips along the side, swirled her tongue around my head, working me into a frenzy. I struggled to maintain control, not wanting to finish too soon.

228

A wedge-shaped cushion lay beside us, catching my eye. I pressed my hand against Jackie's cheek to halt her movements and placed the cushion on the mattress. Without a word, I grasped the back of her hair and bent her over the wedge, pressing her head into the mattress.

"Open those gorgeous thighs of yours."

She spread her legs wide, revealing her bare sex. I'd craved her since that first party. Kneeling behind her, I guided my cock to her entrance and thrust myself in as hard as I could. She let out a quiet cry as I bottomed out inside her. I grabbed her hair again, pulling her head back as I fucked her mercilessly.

My balls slapped against her clit, already slick with her nectar. She tried to look back at me. "That's it, fuck me hard! Own that pussy!"

Her filthy words shocked me but turned me on even more, and I fucked her just as she asked. Wanting to savor this passionate moment, I pulled out and slid my cock up to her ass, then back down, spreading her juices over her tight star.

She looked back and grinned. "Normally, I'd love to get fucked in the ass, but I didn't really prepare for that tonight."

I didn't argue, just rolled her onto her back, positioning her ass on top of the wedge. Then I opened her legs wide and buried my cock inside her again. My body burned with desire, and her fluttering eyelids told me she felt the same. With her hips elevated, I drove into her deeper and faster.

"I'm close, keep fucking me!"

I kept going, reaching forward to wrap my hands around her throat. She placed her hands over mine, holding them in place. I squeezed a little harder as I thrust, and she screamed, "I'm coming!" Her eyes rolled back.

Her loud exclamation and the way her pussy clenched around me pushed me over the edge. I came hard, filling her with everything I had.

She reached down, wiped some of my cream with her fingers, and put it in her mouth. "Mmm. Just the way I remember."

I stared in awe at her seductive display.

Then she asked, "Do you and Ginger have a condom rule?"

Shit. Why was she only asking now? Why hadn't I thought about it?

"Don't worry about me," she said. "I'm all negative and fixed, so no worries, but I don't want you to get in trouble with your wife."

"Yeah, we have that rule, but we've found that many of our initial rules are sort of falling to the wayside."

She laughed. "This can be fun without so many rules. Let's get dressed and join the party."

Ginger

Ryan came back with Jackie with a Cheshire cat grin. Jackie thanked me and walked off to meet some other friends.

Ryan looked so happy that I asked, "I take it she rocked your world?"

He replied, "Oh yes, she did!"

I smiled up at him and raised my eyebrows. "Who's the best wife in the world?"

He smirked and put his arm around me. "Thank you so very much for being a fantastic wife."

I gave him a brief kiss. "Thank you for realizing it."

We joined Kurt, Maryann, and several others, who'd formed a circle on the dance floor.

"If you can find some peppermint schnapps, I'll let you give me a shot," I told Ryan, looking over at the ice sculpture.

His eyes lit up. "I'll be right back." He quickly returned with a whole bottle of peppermint schnapps. I didn't ask how he got it. "Okay, ladies," he said, holding it up. "Let's put some lips on some lips."

I laughed and playfully slapped his arm. We had a small following as we walked to the ice sculpture. They must have seen the bottle Ryan had lifted from somewhere.

The poor, dripping girl had obviously been in the warm air for a while, but it seemed her parts were still in good working order. I leaned back and placed my mouth between her thighs as Ryan poured a quick shot in her mouth.

Then I pulled my head up, swallowed, and said, "Next."

Maryann was next, and a few other ladies followed. Then the guys each took a shot. I looked at Ryan and leaned my head back.

"Another one?" he asked.

"Are you actually questioning my desire to put my mouth on a pussy?"

He pumped his fist and grinned, then poured another shot down the sculpture's mouth. I received it, swallowed, and laughed.

Ryan kissed me. "Damn, I love you."

"I love you too. Now take me to bed and fuck my brains out!"

We said our goodbyes to everyone and went up to our room, where Ryan took very good care of my needs, as I did his. We lay there, talking for a little while about the party and the friends we'd met, before we fell asleep.

Chapter 19: The Inquisition

Ryan

A few evenings later, we gathered with Chet and Mercedes on their back porch, nursing a few bottles of wine. The night air was cool, the kind that made the wine taste better, and their porch lights cast a soft glow over our faces. Mercedes and Ginger, always close, sat together, their heads almost touching as they whispered about mundane events in their lives.

Ginger had been itching to share our new lifestyle with Mercedes, but her friend's conservative side kept her lips sealed. We kept the conversation light, diving into local politics, town happenings, and tossing around half-baked business ideas.

Mercedes leaned forward, a curious glint in her eye. "You guys go out a lot on weekends. Where do you go?"

Ginger tensed beside me. "Remember our friends Jack and Deedee?" I said, trying to keep my voice casual. "We've gone out with them and their friends a few times." Her shoulders relaxed, her smile returning.

"And how do you know Jack and Deedee again?" Chet asked, his tone far too innocent.

My heart pounded. "We met them at the Hitching Post a while back and hit it off really well," I replied, meeting Mercedes's gaze.

She scrutinized me, her eyes narrowing as if searching for cracks in my story.

Ginger jumped in. "We should invite them to join us sometime for wine. They enjoy many of the same things we do."

Mercedes tilted her head, a slow smile forming. "Yeah, that would be great. We'd love to meet them sometime."

Crisis averted, for now. But Mercedes's piercing gaze suggested she wasn't entirely convinced.

We continued sipping our wine, jokes and laughter filling the air. But I couldn't shake the feeling of being watched. Mercedes kept glancing at Ginger, suspicion etched on her face.

Ginger broke the tension first. "I think I need to get some sleep. I've got a big workload in the morning, and this wine will definitely give me a headache if I stay out too late."

Chet nodded. "Glad you could stop by. It's great to catch up."

Mercedes reached out to touch Ginger's arm. "I'm sorry if it came across like I was prying. I was just curious about what you're up to these days."

Ginger gave her a big hug, and to my surprise, Mercedes kissed her on the lips. My heart skipped a beat. That was new.

After Ginger hugged Chet, we said our goodbyes and walked home in silence. Our usual night routine felt strained, the air thick with unspoken words. Coffee set up, dishes loaded, doors locked, teeth brushed—all done in silence.

234

As we lay in bed, Ginger finally spoke. "It's been eating me alive not to say anything. I think Mercedes knows about us. The way she looked at us tonight, it was like she wanted us to confess something, or that *she* wanted to confess."

I chuckled, trying to lighten the mood. "Well, I did notice the kiss she gave you."

Ginger turned to face me, her eyes wide. "Did you see that? She's never kissed me on the mouth before. I think she knows and wants us to tell them. Do you think they're interested?"

"Maybe, but we can't take that risk. We can't lose them as friends."

We agreed to keep our secret, unwilling to jeopardize our friendship with Chet and Mercedes. The stories of friendships ruined by such revelations haunted us. Yet, curiosity about Mercedes lingered in the back of my mind.

#

Weeks passed, and our involvement in the lifestyle dwindled to occasional checks on SLS. We spent more evenings with Chet and Mercedes, their earlier curiosity seemingly forgotten.

One weekend, Mercedes brought up Ginger's upcoming birthday. "It's your fortieth. Got anything fun planned?"

Before Ginger could respond, I jumped in. "We were planning a nice dinner out, just the two of us."

Ginger raised an eyebrow at me as if surprised. We hadn't discussed it, but I had ideas.

Mercedes pouted. "Oh, we would have loved to help you celebrate. I don't know what Ryan has in mind, but I can imagine."

No, she really couldn't.

Ginger smiled. "My birthday is on a Saturday. We could go out with you two on Friday."

"That would work out great," I added, relieved.

"Okay, sounds like a plan," Chet said, his smile genuine.

We toasted to the upcoming celebration, the air lightening, but the unspoken tension remained a constant undercurrent to our friendship.

We enjoyed the rest of the evening with our dearest friends, laughing and talking about our lives. There was nothing they didn't know about us. Well, almost nothing. After a couple bottles of wine and some appetizers, we went home.

As Ginger and I got ready for bed, she asked, "When were you going to tell me your plans for my birthday?"

"I was talking with Kurt and thought we would help you celebrate, but we never discussed any details."

She frowned. "Are you doing all this behind my back? Don't I have a say?"

"Sweetie, there isn't anything planned yet. It was just an idea. Of course I would discuss it with you, but I also thought having a lifestyle birthday celebration for you would be pretty fun."

Ginger hesitated. "Well, we'll see. Please don't make any plans without me. I would get too nervous."

I agreed.

As we always did, we kissed each other good night, I put my arm around Ginger, and off to sleep we went.

Chapter 20: A Very Happy Birthday

Ginger

Over the next couple of months, Ryan and I stayed swamped with work, but we carved out time to regularly attend a local lifestyle meet and greet. These events let like-minded adults mingle over drinks and get to know each other. If sparks flew, they'd swap contact info for a private rendezvous later. We met plenty of fun new friends and spent time with Kurt, Maryann, Jack, and Deedee, who all attended regularly. Their introductions connected us with so many others.

One evening, during a meet and greet, Kurt, Maryann, Ryan, and I discussed my upcoming birthday plans. Kurt joked about having some birthday rope with my name on it. We laughed until Ryan chimed in, "Ginger's expressed interest in making out with forty men for her fortieth birthday."

Mortification surged through me. I couldn't believe he shared that. I slapped his knee and gulped my beer.

Kurt's devilish grin widened. "Is that right?"

I stayed silent, but my crimson cheeks spoke volumes.

"I think we can help with that birthday wish," Kurt announced, then bellowed, "Who wants to help celebrate Ginger's birthday?"

Surprisingly, everyone raised their glasses. Embarrassment and anger swirled within me. Ryan had promised to coordinate with me first. I was unsure if I was okay with this, so I didn't want to make a scene.

Kurt then asked Ryan if we could host the party at our house. I gripped Ryan's hand firmly. "Dear, can I have a word with you outside?"

"Uh-oh," Kurt said, eyes narrowing. "Is there something wrong?"

"No, just a quick discussion before we make any commitments," I replied, forcing a smile.

Outside, I dragged Ryan around the corner, out of sight. "You said you'd coordinate with me. How could you do this?" Anxiety clawed at my chest.

Ryan tried to soothe me, hands on my arms. "Sweetie, I didn't know he was going to do that. He acted without coordinating with me too."

I searched Ryan's eyes and found sincerity. "What do we do now?"

He shrugged. "It's up to you. We'll have an empty house that can handle many friends."

Taking a deep breath, I nodded. "Okay, fine. Let's do it. But no surprises. Be honest with me."

We walked back inside.

"Is everything all right?" Kurt said. "I should have asked you first, but I thought this would prevent you from saying no."

I laughed. "If you want me to suck your dick ever again—without biting it off—don't pull that stunt again."

239

Laughter rippled through us. I agreed to the party.

"Great, I'll handle the invitations," Kurt said, then added, "with your approval, of course."

I smiled, relieved. "Thank you."

Throughout the rest of the evening, people approached me, but my mind raced as everything quickly unfolded.

Tony and Lana, new friends from the last party, approached us first. Lana grinned, offering to help set up for the party. Maryann soon joined us, enthusiastically offering her assistance too. I pulled them both into a hug.

"I'm not sure about this," I confessed, my voice barely steady.

Maryann tightened her embrace. "It'll be fine. We'll only invite people we know and trust. No Creepy Guys, I promise."

I chuckled, remembering that first party we'd attended.

"We have three weeks to plan. It should be fun," Lana added.

After a while, I turned to Ryan. "Can we leave early?"

He nodded, and we began our goodbyes, exchanging kisses and hugs with everyone. We soon found Kathy and her boyfriend, whom we'd met a couple of months ago.

"I'm sorry we missed your party. How did it go?" I asked.

"We ended up postponing it," Kathy replied. "We're rescheduling it to next month. Maybe you can make it then?"

"Sorry, but we're not sure. We don't like to commit unless we're confident we can show up. We always want to be reliable."

Kathy nodded, understanding. She gave us the new date and hugged us both. Then I briefly hugged her boyfriend, who was a man of few words. Ryan's kiss to Kathy lingered longer than expected.

As we neared the door, Kurt's voice boomed behind us. "Party at Ryan and Ginger's three Saturdays from now!"

I spun around, baring my teeth at Kurt in a mock snarl. He got the message, grabbed himself, and grinned.

I laughed, looking around at the cheering crowd. "It starts at seven!" I announced.

Cheers erupted around us, and that's when it hit me.

I was in way over my head.

#

Ten days before my birthday, Ryan and I decided to attend the weekly M&G. Usually, there were five to ten couples at these gatherings, but when we walked in, I was stunned to see closer to twenty couples mingling. We weren't about to wait for a waitress in this crowd, so we grabbed drinks at the bar.

We moved through the room, greeting a few familiar faces. Greetings in this crowd were far more intimate than in our vanilla world—long kisses, occasional ass grabs, chest rubs. I relished these moments, finding them one of the best parts of our lifestyle.

We found Kurt and Maryann. Kurt grinned. "Great turnout, isn't it?"

I nodded. "Yeah, but why so many people? What's going on?"

"They all want to meet you before your birthday party," he replied.

My eyes widened. Fear and anger surged through me. "Everyone here wants to come to our house party?"

Kurt nodded. "Yup, but not all of them will get invited."

I bristled. "Do I get a say in who attends and who doesn't?" I glanced at his crotch with the urge to assert my frustration. "I'm suddenly in the mood to bite down on something."

Kurt, unfazed, wrapped an arm around me and grinned with confidence. "Relax, honey. You can decide who doesn't get an invite. Trust me a little."

I looked between Kurt and Ryan. With a heavy sigh, I conceded. "Okay. We'll make the best of it."

Kurt introduced us to several new couples, who all seemed enthusiastic about the upcoming party. Mark and Debbie offered to bring their portable sex swing.

"Sure," I said, intrigued. "I saw it set up at your house, and I'm curious."

"Maybe it'll be a *very* happy birthday for you," Kurt teased.

I laughed and nudged him. "Go ahead and invite them, but if anyone gets out of control, you'll be the one to kick them out."

Kurt laughed and agreed. Lana approached Ryan with a sly grin. She and Tony were younger than us. Lana and I had quickly become friends, sharing lunches and candid conversations. But why couldn't she talk to me about whatever she was discussing with Ryan?

I walked over, suspicion brewing. "What's going on?"

"Nothing," Ryan said too quickly. "Lana was just asking what we needed for the party."

I didn't buy it, but I played along. "Okay, can you come early to help set up?"

"Sure," Lana said. "I was hoping to help out earlier in the day so you're not stressed before the party."

She was so thoughtful. We continued socializing, and before I knew it, it was 10:00 p.m. With work starting at 7:00 a.m., it was time to leave. Saying goodbye took a while with all the kissing, but as I said, I truly enjoyed this part.

#

The days leading up to the party swarmed with stress. The idea of hosting a gathering of sex enthusiasts in

243

my home gnawed at my nerves. What would our neighbors think? What if they overheard us? What if the police showed up? My mind spiraled with what-ifs until I found ways to distract myself to stave off a full-blown anxiety attack.

Ryan, on the other hand, seemed utterly unfazed. He had faced intense stress in the military and shared countless harrowing stories.

One mission, a nineteen-hour flight, stuck with me. They had been three hours from base, navigating thunderstorms over an ocean dotted with no-fly islands, grappling with fuel issues and faulty cabin pressure that had forced them to use oxygen periodically.

After surviving such ordeals, Ryan claimed nothing on the ground could truly stress him. Maybe if I'd faced those situations, I wouldn't get worked up over much either. But I hadn't, so I did.

The day before the party, I was cleaning the house when a knock interrupted me. I put down the mop and opened the door to find Mercedes with a bright smile on her face.

"Hey, Mercedes! What brings you over?" I asked, trying to sound casual.

"I wanted to see where you wanted to go tonight," she said.

Tonight? Oh my God, I'd completely forgotten about our plans to go out with Chet and Mercedes for my birthday.

"You remembered, right?" Mercedes pressed.

"Of course!" I lied quickly. "I thought Ryan coordinated with you."

"No, he didn't. So, where do you want to go? I know a great Italian place in the new part of town."

"That sounds perfect. Should we meet you there?"

"We can pick you up. That way you can just relax," she said, turning to leave. "We'll be here around six."

"Great, see you then!" I waved as she drove off, then muttered, "Shit!"

I called Ryan, but he didn't answer. Glancing at the clock, I realized he should be on his way home.

He walked in about ten minutes later, barely inside the door before I blurted, "Did you remember we're going out with Chet and Mercedes tonight?"

He must have seen the panic in my eyes. "I actually forgot, but we can still go out."

"Mercedes stopped by and said they'll pick us up at six. I'm freaking out."

Ryan pulled me into a reassuring hug. "Relax, sweetie. We'll have a great time tonight, and tomorrow will be fine too. Our friends are coming early to help set up, and the house looks great."

Six o'clock came too quickly. We were upstairs when we heard a knock followed by Mercedes's voice. "Are you ready?"

Ryan headed down to greet them while I stared at my reflection in the mirror. What am I doing? My stomach churned with worry about tomorrow's party and fear of losing our best friends if they discovered our secret. I wasn't sure I could handle it.

Mercedes's voice rang out. "Come on, Ginger, we have reservations."

Descending the stairs, I spotted Mercedes, who grinned from ear to ear. "Wow, you look gorgeous!" she exclaimed.

I couldn't help but smile back. I wore a knee-length black-and-white plaid skirt paired with a cream blouse and black pumps. My hair fell in soft curls around my shoulders.

Mercedes turned her attention to Ryan. "I hope you told her she looks beautiful."

I tilted my head toward him, clearly indicating he hadn't.

He quickly responded, "Sweetie, you are the most beautiful thing every morning and every evening of my life."

"Uh-huh . . . good recovery," Mercedes said with a smirk.

Chet checked his watch. "If we don't get going, we'll be late for our reservations."

We piled into their car and headed to the restaurant, a place brimming with old-world Italian charm. The ambient music, warm lighting, and stunning art drew me in immediately. The hostess led us to our table, and Mercedes promptly ordered a bottle of wine, choosing with the confidence of a connoisseur.

"All the food here is great. We haven't had anything we didn't like yet," Chet assured us as we perused the menu.

Everything sounded delightful, but I settled on lasagna, a favorite of mine. Ryan chose the veal Parmesan. As the wine flowed and conversation picked up, it felt as if no time had passed since our last gathering. We chatted easily, the pause between our last meeting and tonight seamlessly bridged.

The food surpassed my expectations, each bite bursting with flavor, and the wine paired perfectly. We ordered another bottle and lingered long after our plates were cleared, soothed by the gentle trickle of a nearby water feature and the soft background music.

Mercedes leaned in, her eyes full of concern. "Are you relaxed?"

"Yes, I am, thank you," I replied.

"When I stopped by earlier, you seemed under a lot of stress. Is everything all right?"

"Yeah, it's fine. I've been a little frazzled with work lately," I admitted, which was not a complete lie.

Turning to Ryan, Mercedes asked, "So, where are you taking your lovely bride for her birthday?"

He grinned mischievously. "It's a secret."

"I've been trying to get hints from him all week, and he won't tell me," I added, hoping she'd believe it.

"Okay, but you need to let me know afterward," she insisted.

The rest of the evening flowed without any probing questions, allowing me to fully unwind, free from my earlier stress.

After dropping us back home, Chet and Mercedes stepped out to give me a hug and another kiss, wishing me a happy birthday before driving off. Ryan and I went inside.

"Did you have a good evening?" Ryan asked.

"I did, thank you. I needed that distraction," I replied.

We climbed the stairs and soon fell asleep, the night's warmth lingering in my thoughts.

#

At eight o'clock the next morning, Ryan and I sat on the back porch, sipping coffee and hashing out the day's plan. Most of the prep was done. We just needed to grab ice, mixers like soda and juice, and some bottled water. Ryan got dressed and headed out to fetch those items while I stayed back to set up tables and serving trays.

Tony and Lana arrived around one, hauling a few decorations and a hefty duffel bag. I raised an eyebrow. "What's in the bag?"

Tony grinned. "It's our toy bag."

Wow, I could fit all my toys in a makeup bag. What kind of toys need a duffel bag? "Okayyyy," I said, my voice dripping with skepticism.

Tony laughed, heading upstairs. Lana draped her arm around me. "What can I do to help?"

A short time later, Kurt and Maryann showed up. Maryann asked, "Do you have wash towels in the bathrooms?"

"Of course. I always have one in the bathroom."

She smiled, shaking her head. "Wash towels, plural. People will want to clean up after, and they won't want to share a washcloth."

I hadn't thought of that. Maryann immediately sent Kurt to the discount store for more washcloths.

Before Kurt left, he turned back. "How are we on condoms?"

I gaped at him. "We need to provide condoms too?"

"The host usually keeps them in the bedrooms just in case, but most bring their own," Kurt replied. "Don't worry, I'll get some."

Just when I thought I had everything under control. What else was I missing? Maybe I was in over my head with this party. We'd only been to a couple of these events, and I was sure there were more lessons to learn.

Then Mark and Debbie walked in, lugging a bag that clanged with the sound of metal pipes.

Debbie kissed me on the cheek. "Hi, sweetie. We brought the swing. Where should we set it up?"

"How big is this thing?" I had only seen it briefly at their place.

Mark replied, "It's about six feet by six feet."

"Follow Ryan. He'll find a spot."

249

Mark and Ryan went upstairs to set up the swing. It was 6:00 p.m., and I needed to get ready.

On my way to change, I passed Ryan and Mark as they finished the swing setup. It was a large, framed contraption with four legs and supports. A big spring hung down from the top, holding a seat.

"What are those loops dangling there?" I asked.

"Those are the stirrups," Mark said.

I laughed and walked away, shaking my head.

Lana and Maryann joined me as I got ready. I hopped into the shower, and when I stepped out, there they were, stark naked, putting on makeup in front of my wall mirror.

I toweled off, stealing glances at them. I'd never had two other naked women getting ready for a party with me. *Wow . . . I sure have changed.*

Laughing to myself, I moved to the counter to do my own makeup and hair. Then came my constant dilemma: What to wear?

Thankfully, Maryann and Lana were there to help me decide. I settled on a short ivory dress with a low-cut top that showed off my cleavage. Unlike some of my friends, it took a little more effort to show off my girls.

Then the doorbell rang. I looked at my watch. Seven o'clock on the dot. I stared at myself in the mirror. "Okay, I can do this," I said aloud.

Maryann and Lana both put their arms around me and said, "Breathe, Ginger. It'll be fun."

250

We walked downstairs to see three couples had arrived.

"You look gorgeous," Ryan said. "Just try to relax."

I gave him a kiss. "Game on," I said.

We laughed, kissed each other again, and walked in to chat with our guests. More couples began to arrive, and they brought an assortment of snacks: mixed fruit, cookies, barbecue meatballs, cupcakes, vegetable platters, chicken nuggets, and other similar dishes.

Everyone seemed to simply work their own drinks and socialize with everyone else. It almost seemed to run on auto-party mode. People came in, the wife would find a place to put their dish, the husband would set their coats down and get drinks for the two of them, and then they would mingle. I was surprised by how little effort I needed to make at that point aside from just talking to people.

We soon had about twenty-five couples at the party, and many already knew each other. Everyone was getting along, and after an hour, a few women were already topless. I saw a couple walk upstairs who I didn't think arrived together.

Success! This was going much smoother than I'd thought.

Ryan

Ginger and I broke away to mingle with our guests separately. I'd catch her eye across the room and we'd exchange smiles, a silent check-in to ensure all was well. Lana approached me, her eyes gleaming with mischief.

251

"I'm planning to hijack Ginger," she said, leaning in close. "Some of the girls and I have a surprise for her upstairs. How do you think we should get her up there?"

I scanned the room and spotted Craig, who stood near the drinks. We had met Craig at another social before and Ginger was smitten with him eve since. "Ginger is into him. Ask him to help. But be warned, she's not fond of surprises."

Lana giggled, planting a quick kiss on my cheek. "We'll make up for the surprise part. This is going to be so much fun. Thanks!"

As she flitted away, I locked eyes with Janet. She held my gaze, a sultry smile playing on her lips as she sauntered toward me, her unwavering focus drawing me in. When she reached me, she placed her hands on my chest.

"I don't think I got a proper hello from you yet," she purred.

I grinned and wrapped my arms around her. "How can we fix that?"

Janet took my hand and led me to the now empty dining room. She turned to face me, lifting her skirt to reveal she wore no panties. Hopping onto the wooden table, she spread her legs, her voice low and commanding. "You can start by fucking me."

She unfastened my belt and pants with practiced ease. My mind swam, captivated by her boldness. As she pushed my pants down, I felt the surge of arousal.

"I don't have a condom," I muttered, searching my pockets.

252

She cupped my face, her breath hot against my ear. "You've had a vasectomy, right?"

"Yes, but Ginger and I—"

"No STIs here," she interrupted, pulling me closer. "If you're fixed, fuck me. Now."

Her urgency was contagious. I thrust into her, her wet heat enveloping me. She pulled my mouth to hers, and we kissed fiercely, our bodies moving in sync. She placed my hands on her throat, a reminder of her preference. I tightened my grip, thrusting harder as her pleasure mounted.

"Choke me harder," she gasped, her eyes locked onto mine.

I obliged, feeling her body tremble as she neared climax. She came with a gush, and I followed, groaning loudly. Our shared ecstasy echoed through the empty room.

Janet laughed breathlessly, kissing me. "That was incredible."

"Umm. Ahem."

Kurt's voice broke through the haze. I turned to see him standing awkwardly. "If you're done, we should probably get Ginger's birthday going."

Janet hopped off the table, smoothing her skirt. "Go take care of your wife's birthday. I'll clean up."

I headed toward the doorway, pulling up my pants. I paused to glance back at Janet, who caught my stare and blew me a kiss.

"Go celebrate, or I won't let you fuck me again," she teased.

I chuckled, shaking off the remnants of lust. I stepped into the living room, ready to gather everyone for the main event.

Ginger

Ryan climbed onto a cooler, commanding everyone's attention. My stomach churned with anxiety and curiosity. What was he up to now?

Kurt sidled up to me with a wide grin. "We have a present for you," he said with mischief dancing in his eyes.

Nervous energy surged through me. What had these guys schemed?

"Hello, everyone!" Ryan's voice boomed over the crowd. "Thanks for coming to celebrate Ginger's fortieth birthday!"

Cheers erupted, filling the room with excitement.

"I'm here to ask for your help with a special request she made." He paused, letting the anticipation build. "One thing she wanted was to make out with forty men for her fortieth birthday. We might not have exactly forty men, but we've got plenty of willing participants. She'll be in the living room, blindfolded, with her hands bound. Let's make her birthday wish come true!"

My heart raced with shock, and a thrill coursed through me. Kurt guided me into the living room, his touch steady and reassuring. "Trust me," he murmured, slipping a blindfold over my eyes and tying my hands behind my back.

"Okay, everyone, form a line," Kurt instructed the crowd. "Fifteen seconds each. We can't do this all night."

My body trembled with nerves. Kurt's voice softly whispered in my ear, "Relax and go with it, sweetie. You'll have fun."

The first kiss landed on my lips, firm and confident. His tongue slipped into my mouth, exploring, teasing. Just as I started to lose myself in the kiss, I heard, "Next!"

Softer lips met mine, probably a woman this time. Each kiss brought a new sensation, some gentle, others rough. Hands roamed over my breasts, adding an erotic thrill. I experienced a heady mix of disbelief and excitement that I was actually doing this.

My body tingled with euphoria, the differences in kisses from men and women blending into a symphony of sensations. Lingering, soft kisses. Rough, urgent ones. Wet kisses with plenty of tongue. Gentle nibbles on my lips. The longer it lasted, the wetter I became. I wasn't sure how much more I could take, each kiss leaving me yearning for the next. Time seemed to blur.

Finally, the rope loosened from my wrists and the blindfold slipped off. I blinked a few times, my eyes adjusting to the sudden brightness. Ryan stood before me. I lunged at him, our lips crashing together, and I took in his familiar taste and touch. My whole body trembled, and my legs grew weak. He held me up as a powerful orgasm washed over me. I couldn't believe it. I had come just from kissing, each encounter building to this peak.

After I caught my breath, Ryan picked me up and hugged me tightly. "Happy birthday, sweetie."

I needed a drink to steady myself. I made my way to the cooler to grab a beer and some fruit. As I walked through the crowd, everyone smiled at me, and I couldn't help but wonder whose lips had matched each kiss. As I replayed the moments in my mind, my arousal ramped up again, the memories of each kiss lingering on my lips.

When I finally found Ryan, he was engrossed in conversation with an attractive brunette. As I approached, she broke into a smile and hugged me warmly.

"Happy birthday, Ginger! I don't think we've formally met, other than my kissing you . . . er . . . twice." She looked guilty but continued, "I'm Sherry. I'm so happy to be here. You two are such gracious hosts."

I reached up and pulled her into another kiss. The moment our lips met, I handed my drink to Ryan, Sherry's lips incredibly soft against mine. Her hands slipped inside the top of my dress, and I instantly remembered those hands too.

I gradually pulled away, breathless. "Wow! Thank you for coming to my party."

We laughed together, and Sherry and I took our drinks back from Ryan, who stood there, stunned.

"You can close your mouth now," I teased, and we all laughed again.

Then a man who I'd noticed earlier approached me. Rarely am I immediately smitten by someone, but he was an exception. He had dark hair, dark eyes, and an olive complexion, and was a bit shorter than Ryan.

"Hi, I'm Craig. My wife Theresa is by the bar." He pointed, and a petite redhead waved at me. "Happy birthday, Ginger," he said, leaning in to kiss me.

My pulse quickened. I needed to be fucked right now, and he seemed to sense my desire.

"Would you like to go upstairs?" he whispered.

His forwardness caught me off guard, but excitement bubbled up. "Yes!" I exclaimed, maybe too eagerly.

Damn, was I too quick? Should I have talked to him more? I barely knew this guy, and here I was, ready to have sex with him.

I laughed to myself. What have I become?

Craig took my hand, and we climbed the stairs to my bedroom. Inside, Lana stood by the bed with five other women, all in gorgeous negligees. I recognized Deedee, Terra, and Maryann, and the other two from other parties. Then I noticed the four restraints at each corner of the bed.

I turned to Craig, confused. "Um, what's going on?"

He ducked his head, looking apologetic. "I am so very sorry. They made me do it." He slipped back into the hall, leaving me with the women and the waiting restraints.

Lana clasped my hand, her touch firm and deliberate as she led me toward the bed. "We have a surprise for you," she said, her voice low and inviting. She took my drink and placed it on the nightstand with a soft clink. The other women closed in, their hands cool against my skin as they undressed me, their lips grazing my flesh with gentle, lingering kisses. My initial nervousness ebbed away, replaced by a growing warmth.

With my clothes discarded in a pile, they guided me to the bed. Four women secured the restraints around my wrists and ankles, the leather cool and snug. Lana placed a blindfold over my eyes and whispered, "Relax and enjoy."

Was this what they'd had in that duffel bag? Curious and excited, I wondered what they'd planned. I had experimented with toys before and was ready for a new adventure.

Their mouths moved over my body, kissing my lips, and then my nipples, and trailed downward until—there it was: a tongue on my slick folds. I tugged at the restraints, my back arching instinctively.

"She likes this," someone murmured.

I laughed breathlessly. "I do so far."

A humming sound filled the air, unmistakable and thrilling. The vibration touched my breasts first, softer and different from anything I'd felt before. It wasn't like my trusty Bob. Then it descended to my core.

"Whoa!" I gasped, my muscles involuntarily clenching, my limbs jerking against the restraints. "That's intense."

They kept it there, teasing me until I shattered, the orgasm ripping through me. The restraints strained as I pulled against them, lost in the overwhelming pleasure. The vibration ceased, replaced by a warm mouth, a tongue sliding up my sensitive slit. My back arched again. This was beyond anything I'd ever experienced. Something soft traced my body, circled my nipples, tickled my neck, while hands and lips explored every inch of my skin. I was a live wire, every nerve electrified.

The humming resumed, and Lana's voice cut through the haze. "Open her up for me."

Two hands slid over my mound, parting my swollen lips. Something vibrated as it entered me, slow and tantalizing. The intensity grew, a buzz on my little pearl. It reminded me of the toy Ryan and I had used, the one that broke in the car.

The pleasure was unreal, each sensation blending into the next. They kissed and touched and fucked me with the toy, driving me to another climax that tore through me, a cry escaping my lips. If not for the restraints, I would have flailed. This orgasm was even more forceful, leaving me breathless.

"Let me go!" I cried, my voice raw. The restraints fell away, and I curled into a ball, my body trembling with aftershocks. Voices murmured around me, but all I could focus on was the intensity, the lingering pleasure.

Finally, I relaxed, removed the blindfold, and stretched out on the bed. The girls lay around me, their faces gleeful, their mission accomplished.

"Happy birthday, Ginger!" they chorused.

Wow. What a birthday.

When I stood up, my legs wobbled, threatening to collapse beneath me. Craig, the guy who had led me upstairs, caught me just in time. His strong hands steadied me, and I couldn't help but feel a spark of gratitude.

As I slipped into a sheer lace nightie, I glanced up at him. "So, Benedict Arnold, were you watching me?"

His cheeks flushed a deep crimson. "Oh yes, I did. You don't mind, do you?"

A part of me reveled in his admission. He had just watched me get ravaged by five women, and now he was blushing. I wanted him anyway, so what could I say?

"No, I don't mind, but I need a quick break. Come find me in thirty minutes, and we can pick up where we left off."

He kissed me, his lips lingering on mine, before I headed downstairs. I needed something to drink and eat. Sex drained my energy, and I'd learned that fruit was perfect for replenishing it and getting the motor running again.

I scanned the room for Ryan, hoping he was having as much fun as I was. Then I made my way back upstairs, curiosity guiding me. All the bedroom doors were closed, and air mattresses in the open areas were occupied. Our house had turned into a playground of desire.

I almost missed seeing Craig's wife, Theresa, naked on the floor, riding someone. She turned, her eyes meeting mine, and smiled. It took me a second to recognize the person beneath her—Ryan.

I watched them for a moment. Theresa moved sensually, sliding up and down on Ryan's shaft, her body responding to his touch. His hands roamed her curves, and I could tell he was thoroughly enjoying himself. Theresa seemed equally pleased. I noticed he wore a condom. Good boy.

I knelt beside Ryan, kissed him, then moved to Theresa. "Don't let him go until you're completely satisfied," I said.

She laughed. "Oh, he's satisfied me twice already. This is just a bonus."

"Great. That's all he needs for his ego."

We laughed, and I let them continue. I returned downstairs for more food and water, finding a plate of fruit and some chocolate, when Sherry approached me.

"This party is great! We should get together again soon," she exclaimed.

We chatted for a bit until my cell phone rang. I excused myself and saw it was Mercedes who was calling.

A million thoughts raced through my head as I found a quiet spot. "Hi, Mercedes."

"Hi, Ginger. I'm sorry to bother you. Are you still out?"

I hesitated. "Yes, we're still out, but heading home soon. What's up?"

"I think your daughter is having a party at your house. There are about twenty cars here. Do you want me to go over and break it up?"

My heart skipped a beat. "I'll call her and tell her to send everyone home. We should be back in an hour."

"Okay. I hope your evening is going well. Where did Ryan take you?"

Damn, she's fishing. "A nice steak and seafood restaurant."

"Sounds fancy. Okay, have a great night. Good luck with the kids."

I hung up, staring at the phone. Damn, I needed a shot. I walked over to the bar and announced, "Who wants to get me drunk?"

The response was overwhelming. Everyone offered bottles of booze. A very naked Lana stood there with a bottle of my favorite peppermint schnapps.

"I'll take what she has," I said.

A guy next to Lana winked at me. "I've been trying to take what she has all evening."

We all laughed, and Lana replied, "Well, then why haven't you asked?" She handed me the bottle and walked away with him.

I took my shot of schnapps and returned to the kitchen, where Ryan joined me a moment later.

"Mercedes called," I said hurriedly. "She thought our daughter was having a party, so she offered to break it up since she thought we were out. I think I need another shot."

Ryan wrapped his arms around me. "What did you tell her?"

I relayed my conversation with her, each word easing the tension from my shoulders.

"That was good. I'm sure it'll be fine," he assured me.

He was right. It would all be fine. Hopefully.

I wandered around the room, picking up glasses, bottles, and empty food trays. As I reached for another tray, hands snaked around my waist from behind. Craig.

"Well, hello," I said, turning to face him.

He pulled me close and planted a big kiss on my lips. "Are you ready?"

"Lead the way."

I needed a distraction, and Craig was perfect for that. As I scanned the downstairs area, it was eerily empty. The clock showed midnight. Strangely, everyone had left without a word.

"Did everyone leave?" I asked Craig.

"I didn't see anyone leave."

We ascended the stairs, heading to the first open bedroom door. Inside, four couples tangled in a mass of lust. One woman glanced up and invited us to join them.

"Want to?" Craig asked.

"No, I want something private. Just you and me."

We moved to the next bedroom, but the closed door signaled it was occupied. At play parties, opening a closed door was a strict no-no. We entered our large playroom, and the sight took my breath away. Nearly ten couples were scattered around, on air mattresses, couches, the floor, and in a swing. A stunning blonde sat in the swing, legs wide, being pounded by a muscular man. His every muscle rippled with each thrust, and she moaned around another man's cock.

I need one of those swings, I thought.

The room was a sea of intertwined bodies, everyone comfortable with the audience. I felt myself getting wetter as I watched.

"Let's see if another room is open," Craig said, pulling me from my reverie. He took my hand and led the way as I continued to marvel at the scene.

We found an empty bedroom. Craig closed the door behind us, and I set down my drink. He wrapped his arms around me from behind, and his lips found my neck. The scent of his cologne sent a jolt straight to my core. His kisses hit all the right spots, and when he nibbled my ear, I couldn't stifle a moan.

I turned to face him, draped my arms around his neck, and kissed him deeply. He lowered my arms and gradually slid my nightie off my shoulders, letting it pool at my feet. I stood there, completely exposed.

He leaned down and sucked on my breasts, gently biting my nipples. Shivers ran down my spine. I fumbled with his shirt buttons, eager to feel his skin.

264

God, I love a man with a hairy chest.

My fingers traced down his chest and stomach, followed by soft kisses as I sank to my knees. I looked up into his eyes, unbuckling his belt. His mouth hung slightly open, his eyes burning with anticipation. I unzipped his pants, feeling his hardness through the fabric, and pulled them down, revealing his boxers.

My hands roamed up Craig's hairy legs, feeling the coarseness under my fingertips, until they reached his hips. His bulge, straining against his boxers, hovered inches from my mouth. He was undeniably aroused. I kissed his dick through the tented fabric, tracing its outline with my lips. His breathing grew heavier. With deliberate slowness, I tugged at the elastic waistband and peeled his boxers down. His cock sprang free, pointing straight at my mouth.

I licked the tip, savoring the salty taste, and then kissed it before enveloping the head with my lips. He threw his head back, groaning, and then looked down at me. Maintaining eye contact, I cupped his balls with one hand and let him watch as I slid his entire length into my mouth. I felt the tip hit the back of my throat. Pausing, I concentrated and relaxed before pushing it farther.

His cockhead nudged into my throat. He grabbed the back of my head, making me gag. I pulled back, laughing. "If you want that, don't grab my head."

"Sorry, I couldn't help it. No one's ever done that to me before."

Pride flushed my cheeks. I never thought I'd be someone's first in this way. Craig lifted me and laid me back on the bed.

He spread my legs and buried his head between my thighs. His tongue licked up and down my slit before swirling around my clit. My pulse quickened, goose bumps prickling my skin. He knew exactly what he was doing. Just as I teetered on the edge of an orgasm, he stood up. My breath caught, frustration flaring. I really wanted that release. He widened my legs and positioned the tip of his cock at my entrance, his eyes locking onto mine. The anticipation made me ache.

He thrust into me, and I gasped. I'd had sex countless times, but this felt different, more intense. I wrapped my legs around him, matching his rhythm. His cock filled me, and each stroke sent me higher.

"Keep your eyes open," he commanded, his voice a rough whisper.

I opened my eyes and met his hungry gaze. He looked like he was claiming me. Every thrust pushed me closer to the edge. I panted, the heat in my core growing, spreading, consuming me. When it became too much, I screamed as the orgasm crashed over me.

Craig paused, and I cried out, "Don't stop! Keep fucking me!"

He continued, and the orgasm rolled on, my inner walls clenching around him. The head of his cock stroked rhythmically against my G-spot. With a sudden burst, I squirted, drenching him and the bed.

266

I patted his arm, whispering, "Okay."

He stopped, allowing me to catch my breath. Then he knelt down and resumed licking my soaked sex, his tongue moving with torturous slowness. I was hypersensitive now, every touch magnified.

After a moment, he looked up. "Ready?"

I whimpered and nodded. "Mm-hmm."

He spread my legs again and entered me, this time pushing my knees back to my head. He pounded into me, his balls slapping against my ass, and the head of his cock tapping my cervix with each thrust. He leaned down to kiss me, the deeper angle driving me wild.

He took me as he wanted, and I floated in a dimension of pure bliss. After what felt like an eternity, he yelled, "I'm coming!"

His words triggered another orgasm. It wasn't as intense, but I loved feeling his cock pulse inside me as he came. He finished and leaned down to kiss me.

Then realization hit. "You didn't use a condom!"

"You didn't say anything, so I assumed it was okay." His eyes were wide with worry. "I'm sorry. Is it a problem?"

I took a breath. "I'm fixed, so no pregnancy issues. But Ryan and I have a rule about using condoms with others. I should've told you." I sighed. He was right, I hadn't mentioned it. "Don't worry. You're clean, right?"

He nodded. "Theresa and I get tested regularly, and we're careful. No worries there."

Craig lay beside me, gently caressing my breasts. "Thanks for a wonderful night. Sorry about the condom."

I was elated, feeling blissfully satiated. "You're welcome. Don't worry. I needed this tonight." I kissed him. "I have to get back downstairs. People will be leaving soon."

We dressed quickly, the soft rustle of fabric and the faint scent of cologne filling the room. As we walked down the hall, we noticed the near silence. The once lively party had quieted. I craved more of that sweet energy fruit and knew it was definitely water time.

Downstairs, a crowd surrounded the food table, laughter and chatter filling the air as if this were a casual neighborhood gathering. I couldn't help but marvel at the contrast. Just moments ago, these people were upstairs, indulging in passionate encounters. Now they discussed everyday topics, the kind you'd share with neighbors over a cup of coffee.

Oh, the neighbors. My mind raced with the possible rumors. Some of the ladies, myself included, had been quite loud. I hoped the walls had muffled our sounds.

Maryann approached with a wide grin, enveloping me in a big hug. "Great party! Thanks for hosting."

Kurt joined us, his proud grin matching Maryann's. "Fantastic job. Everyone had a blast."

I hugged them both, feeling a rush of gratitude. "Thanks. I couldn't, or probably wouldn't, have done it without you."

We shared a laugh, the truth of my words clear to all of us.

As guests began to leave, we exchanged kisses and thank-yous. Misbuttoned shirts and tousled hair were the norm, but everyone seemed happy as they departed. Kurt, Maryann, Tony, and Lana stayed behind to spend the night. When we returned to the kitchen, the mess hit us like a wave.

"Come on," Maryann said, rolling up her sleeves. "Let's knock this out. Ryan, grab a large trash bag and toss the leftover food."

"It's a shame to waste it all," I protested, eyeing the spread.

"Will you eat everything within the next couple of days?" she asked pointedly.

I sighed, conceding. "No, probably not. Go ahead and dump it."

By the time we finished cleaning, it was three in the morning, and we were all exhausted.

We trudged up to our bedroom. Ryan crawled into bed beside me, his voice a soft murmur. "It was a great party, sweetie. I love you."

I smiled, leaning into him. "I love you too, honey."

We kissed goodnight and fell asleep almost instantly.

#

I awoke to the smell of bacon. Ryan was already gone. I threw on my bathrobe and glanced in the mirror. My hair was a mess, but considering last night's crowd had seen me in worse shape, I shrugged it off and headed downstairs. Everyone was up, working together to make breakfast. Maryann handed me a cup of coffee, and Ryan passed me a breakfast sandwich.

"Good morning, sunshine," Kurt greeted me with a grin.

I sipped my coffee, smiling back. "Good morning, everyone. Thanks for this."

We settled on the back porch, eating and reminiscing about the party. Maryann mentioned they'd cleaned all the rooms, pulled off the sheets, and emptied the wastebaskets. One bed, she noted with a smirk, was especially wet and needed time to dry.

Curious, I asked, "Which one?"

"The small one upstairs, near the swing," she replied.

Heat rushed to my face. "Um, I'll claim responsibility for that," I admitted, flushing even harder as everyone clapped and cheered.

I shushed them with a loud whisper, not wanting the neighbors to hear, and sipped my coffee until the embarrassment faded. We chatted a bit longer, then everyone pitched in to clean up before heading home.

Ryan and I stood at the door in our robes, arms around each other, and kissed when the last car drove off. We spent the rest of the day tidying the house, washing

270

sheets, and storing party supplies. Every time we passed each other, we exchanged grins and sneaky kisses. At one point, Ryan pinned me against the laundry room wall and kissed me deeply.

That evening, I sank into the old wicker chair on the back porch, a glass of chardonnay in hand. The party had been a whirlwind, a kaleidoscope of laughter and music still echoing in my mind. Ryan and I agreed it had been a fantastic success, but a lingering desire to reconnect with our family and vanilla friends tugged at my heart.

"You've been using condoms, right?" I asked, swirling the wine in my glass.

Ryan glanced at me, a sheepish look crossing his face. "Last night, Janet kind of made me go without."

"She forced you against your will, did she?" I teased, trying to mask the guilt gnawing at me.

"What about you?" he countered, his eyes narrowing slightly.

I hesitated, thinking about Craig. "I slipped up once, but that's no excuse. We need to stick to our rule until we get to know someone better."

He gave me the knowing grin that always irked me.

"Okay, you caught me breaking another rule. Now wipe that smirk off your face. Let's just hope nothing bad comes of these mistakes," I said.

We nestled closer, watching the sky bleed orange and pink as the sun dipped below the horizon. My mind wandered, the colors blurring with my thoughts.

"Remember last week when I said that I wanted to spend more time in our vanilla life?" I asked, my voice barely above a whisper. "Let's take a break from this lifestyle for a while. I feel like it's consuming us."

Ryan's brow furrowed. "What do you mean it's 'consuming' us?"

"I love our lifestyle friends, and all the new people we're meeting, but I miss our old life too."

He didn't respond immediately, his gaze fixed on the TV. I tapped his chest, demanding his attention. "Hey, I'm serious."

"I know, baby. I was just thinking about how much fun we're having."

"We are having fun, but it's almost like a drug. We need to find a happy balance."

He nodded, a flicker of understanding in his eyes. "I agree. We should balance it with our other friends and family."

This lifestyle had opened doors we never knew existed. Our new friends were incredible—supportive, nonjudgmental, and above all, fun. They created a space where we could be unapologetically ourselves. Those nontraditional friendships allowed us to experience thrills that titillated our senses and expanded our minds.

Yet, most of our vanilla friends wouldn't understand how swinging could enrich our lives—or theirs. Sharing intimacy with others and returning to each other with renewed excitement and hunger was something they couldn't fathom. I couldn't imagine leaving this lifestyle, but I also missed the simplicity of our vanilla life.

Our new experiences and friends didn't diminish the facets of our vanilla life that we cherished. They were two sides of the same coin, and we needed to find that balance to ensure we could continue to enjoy our secret life. We doubted we could ever explain to our vanilla friends what this lifestyle had done for us, but it was an awakening unlike anything we had ever imagined.

Read other great adventures through the mind of L. T. Richards:

The Firm's Deception

Brett is a young, handsome engineer who wants a career at a prominent firm.

Grace spent her life building an engineering firm, specializing in delivering the exact product her clients want.

What can a young engineer do when he finds out that he may be the product?

Will Brett learn of the firm's deception, or will he succumb to its plan for him?

Our Secret Life: Full Immersion brings Ryan and Ginger's experiences to new heights with current friends and new friends. They find that their longtime vanilla friends are more than curious in their endeavors and in one unplanned evening, they find out how their interests merge. What they didn't expect was their friend's involvement into another lifestyle which drive Ryan and Ginger's explorations to a level they never imagined.